HEX EDUCATION

M.J. CAAN

VINCI
BOOKS

By M.J. Caan

Singing Falls Witches

Hex After Forty
That Good Hex
How Torie Got Her Hex Back
Hex and Chocolate
Moonlight Hexes
Hex and the Single Witch
Hex Education
Hex After Dark
That Hex Factor

For B. The real magic in my life.

Vinci Books

vinci-books.com

Published by Vinci Books Ltd in 2025

1

Printed and bound in Great Britain by Clays Ltd, Elcograf S.p.A.

Chapter One

A single bead of sweat had formed on Torie Bliss' forehead. She peered deeply into the glass, holding her breath, scarcely daring to move in the slightest lest she disturb the powers-that-be whom had gifted her this one perfect creation.

At her side, Jasmin, her best friend and fellow witch, stood ready to assist at a moment's notice. They glanced carefully at one another, each feeding off the other's trepidation.

"So delicate," said Jasmin. "It's barely holding together. I'm not sure this is something we should even be attempting."

Torie shook her head. "No, this is the kind of offering that will put us on the map. I mean we're both good at this, but we need to take our skills to the next level if we're going to really succeed."

"I think we're setting ourselves up for attack with this one. I'm going to leave it to you. I'll find something else to offer up."

Torie didn't respond as she tentatively reached forward, willing her hand not to shake so as not to disrupt the delicate nature of what they had just created.

"Are you sure it's ready?" asked Jasmin, stepping slowly back from her friend.

Torie exhaled sharply, blowing a strand of hair free of her face. "We'll find out."

Carefully, she lifted the pan from the large gas burner of the stove. The large pancake soufflé they had created wiggled menacingly as she slowly moved it to the center island. It was a perfect cream color with an amber top.

"We can't sell this at the bakery," Jasmin said. "It's incredibly hard to make and time consuming."

"It's only hard for us to make because we aren't professional chefs. I'm certain that whoever we hire for the bakery will be able to whip these up in no time. And just think about the press we will get by offering them. No one has anything like this on their menu."

Jasmin looked around the kitchen. "It looks like a food cyclone moved through here. All just to create one pancake."

"It's not *just* a pancake. It's a statement piece. Anyone can make a pancake or a soufflé, but we will be combining the two into a masterpiece that everyone will want to try."

"Who is everyone?" Jasmin asked. "Cos this is Singing Falls. Everyone is going to want their pancakes with a bunch of butter and enough syrup running down them to drown a small child in. Ain't nobody got time for one giant pancake that takes forever to cook and serve." She then eyed the concoction suspiciously. "Now how are you going to get it out of the pan and onto a plate without destroying it? And you can't use magic because the cook most definitely will not be able to."

"Well, it should be set enough now that I can gingerly lift it to its final resting place, and then garnish it with some fresh whipped cream and an edamame thin wafer."

She ignored the look of horror on Jasmin's face as she set about carefully sliding a spatula under the tall cake and lifting it, and the mold it was cooked on, to the plate. Once it was resting, she carefully removed the metal ring from around it.

They both stepped back to admire the creation.

"There," said Torie. "Food as art."

"Well, it does look good," Jasmin replied, moving a little closer.

"It's perfect. Grab a fork and we are going to——"

She was interrupted by the front door opening and closing. Then, a giant box filled with canned goods entered the kitchen, followed by a tiny woman carrying said large box with surprising ease.

"Fionna! Watch out for the——" Jasmin started.

But she was too late. The box was well above Fionna's head, covering her field of vision. She dropped it onto the island, close enough to the pancake that the vibrations caused the soufflé to self-implode.

Torie stared in disbelief at the mound of perfectly whipped eggs and sugar, her fork held high in one hand. Jasmin struggled to contain her giggles, pretending to mourn the cake when Torie looked her way.

"Oh, hey guys," said Fionna, stepping away from the giant box of goods she had slammed down. "I didn't see you there. What's going on?"

She moved to stand next to them, following their eyes to the plate.

"Oh, what's that? Trying out new recipes?" She took the fork from Torie's hand and scooped up some of the flattened pancake and shoveled it into her mouth. "Um…this is good. Reminds me a bit of a pancake. Needs some syrup though."

Jasmin laughed as Torie's eyes flashed a vibrant blue before the magic settled back down within her.

"Did I say something wrong?" Fionna asked, her brown eyes widening above another mouthful of the pancake.

Torie let out a deep sigh. "Nope. Not a thing. So, you really like it?"

The squirrel shifter took another gulp and nodded. "It's a weird consistency, but pretty good." She looked around the kitchen. "What in the world happened in here? I know it didn't take all these dishes and mess to make that one little cake."

Jasmin stepped in, placing a hand on Torie's shoulder to steady her.

"You know, this might be a good time to test out some of the…renovations, we've been making to the house."

"It's a brand-new house," said Fionna. "What could you possibly have done?"

Jasmin offered a mischievous smile and gave her a wink. "It will be easier just to show you."

Torie nodded, and then turned to face the mess of dishes and mixing bowls in the sink, as well as the flour spills and drops of dried batter that decorated the range and countertops. She reached out one hand, twirling her fore-finger in the air as she plucked at the magical threads that floated around the room.

Almost at once, the sink began to fill with water as the dishes began to clean themselves before floating into the waiting dishwasher. The pantry door swung open and a broom that was hanging from the wall danced out and began sweeping the crumbs onto a dustpan before floating to the trash can. Sponges began mopping at the spills on the countertop and the stove, while unused measuring utensils and baking cups rose and returned to their place in the cupboards.

Fionna watched, eyes fixed on the dancing dishes and cleaning tools all around her.

"So, you put a magic whammy on everything and turned it into that movie about that poor indentured girl with the evil stepmother and trashy sisters, huh?"

"What? No. There is no magical whammy. It was a very delicate and multi-layered spell that we cast to make this happen," said Torie.

"Well, it's kind of creepy. Did you enchant the mice and birds to do your laundry?" Fionna asked.

Torie crossed her arms. "Well, that would just be plain silly. Of course not. Besides, Leo ate the only mouse I've seen since moving in."

At the mention of his name, the little dragon zipped into the room, circling around to plop down on Torie's shoulder, his iridescent scales cascading from green to blue to yellow as he huffed into her hair, nuzzling his head against hers.

"Oof. You're getting too big for that," Torie said, reaching up to tickle his sides with her fingers.

"Hello, little Leo," Fionna said, wiggling her fingers at the dragon. His eyes lit up seeing her, and he immediately hopped from Torie's shoulder to run across the island, hopping into Fionna's arms. He folded his wings as she rocked him like a baby. "You just get cuter and cuter every time I see you."

"Huh. He's never that excited to see me," Jasmin said under her breath.

"It's a shifter thing," Fionna responded with a smile.

"Torie's not a shifter," Jasmin huffed.

"No, but she's his mommy. That trumps everything."

"Whatever," Jasmin replied, moving to inspect the giant box that Fionna had brought into the house. "Girl, what is in this?"

"Oh, there was a sale at the restaurant supply store, so I picked up a few things that we are going to need. And since the builders won't be out of the bakery for another week, I thought I'd leave them here until we can start moving stuff in."

"It…takes up a lot of room," said Torie. She reached over to push the box to the side and could barely move it. "Jeez, this thing weighs a ton. How are you just carrying it around like that?"

"Shifter strength," Fionna replied, her smile broadening. "I figure you have so much room here, surely you can find a place where it will be out of the way. And Elric can move it anywhere you need." Her eyes sparkled at the mention of Elric's name. "Speaking of…how are things going with the big, bad wolf?"

Torie cast her a glance out of the corner of her eye as she turned to check on the progress of the magical cleanup. "Things are going great. I couldn't be happier."

"Has he officially moved in?" Fionna asked.

Torie shook her head. "Not yet. But we are getting there."

"Uh oh," said Jasmin, moving to stand next to her friend. "I know that tone. What's wrong?"

Fionna sat Leo down and casually lifted the giant supply box from the island to the floor, so she had an unobstructed view of her friends. "Is something wrong? Between you and Elric?" she asked.

Torie tried to will away the redness she felt creeping up

her neck. There was no point in lying; Jasmin knew her too well, and Fionna had the senses of a lie detector.

Torie offered a wan smile. "Honestly, everything is really good. I have never met a man more attentive, loving, devoted or dedicated to me in my life. He's pretty much perfect."

Jasmin frowned. "No one is perfect, Torie."

"Well, he's pretty darn close, then." She turned back, just as the last dishes marched into the washer and it started itself. She moved to inspect the stove as the sponges finished their cleanup work and headed into the sink to scrub themselves clean. "But I'm not always sure such blind devotion is good for us. I mean, he's like a big old knight in hairy armor; and I don't always need saving."

Both Jasmin and Fionna stared at her, crossing their arms, lips pursed.

"What? You look like you want to say something," Torie said.

"It's just weird hearing you say something like that when you're just as guilty of it as he is," said Fionna.

Torie stared hard at her friend, eyes narrowed. "What are you talking about?"

Jasmin turned and pretended to busy herself with directing the sponges back to their drying racks, and then opening the range door to inspect the inside of Torie's oven. Fionna, eyes narrowed, gave her a steely look before returning her attention to Torie.

"Well…it's just that, you know, you kind of have to be the big protector of everyone you meet. And there is absolutely nothing wrong with that, but you seem to think that you must protect and save everyone. Even if it means striking out on your own to do it."

Torie started to speak but then pursed her lips and

regarded her friend. Leo was sitting up on his hind legs on the island, paying rapt attention to Torie. His emerald-green eyes flicking back and forth between her and the squirrel shifter.

"Sure, I feel a certain responsibility to my friends. Why is that so bad?"

"No one is saying it is," replied Fionna. "It's just that we need you to know that, as strong as you're getting, you don't have to shoulder all the responsibilities for everyone around you. The day is going to come when you're going to have to give in and trust someone else to do the heavy lifting for you."

Torie started to answer but Jasmin interrupted. "Torie, you might just be the strongest hex witch I've ever met, but you can't be everywhere at once. And when that day comes, just know that we'll have your back. And remember, Elric's a good guy. Maybe you guys can learn to cut each other some slack in the who needs to save who category and just…enjoy that you've found one another."

"Speaking of," said Fionna, tilting her head to one side.

A few seconds later, the front door opened and closed again, and Elric walked in, a large bouquet of flowers in one hand. He smiled at everyone and presented them to Torie with a quick peck to her forehead.

"Aww," said Jasmin, giving Torie a knowing glance. "What a good guy."

Elric frowned, but any questions he may have had were smothered as Torie wrapped her arms around him in thanks.

"My big, strong man," she said. "Speaking of, can you please take this to the pantry for me?" She indicated the large box Fionna had brought in.

"Oh, and here I thought you were happy to see all of

me, not just my muscles," he said playfully, picking up the box and heading for the large walk-in pantry that was built off the side of the kitchen.

Torie watched him march off appreciatively. "And where is Max? He is my official taster, and I need his help establishing the new menu." She glanced at Fionna, smiling. "Not that I don't appreciate your appreciation, of course, but Max is very discerning, to say the least."

Like Elric, Max was a werewolf as well. He also happened to be the Sheriff of Singing Falls.

"He got a call just as we were leaving the gym to head over," said Elric.

"Tell me why a werewolf, one of the strongest of the supernaturals, needs to work out?" said Jasmin.

"We don't really need to. But it's a way of strengthening our bond. Physical exertion increases our unique pheromone output which in turn——"

Jasmin held up a hand. "So, you get sweaty and smell each other."

Elric shrugged. "Something like that."

Just then his phone pinged, and he slid it out of his pocket, staring at the message. He looked up, eyes hardened.

"Max just texted. He said he needs us to come meet him at the bus station. A body's been found there; one that he says looks like it needs the kind of attention you specialize in."

Chapter Two

Unlike many small towns across the country, there was no "bad side of town" to Singing Falls. The community was uniformly beautiful, with a thriving downtown main street that bisected a set of graded properties to either side, each of those hosting various businesses and shops away from the lively attractions of main street.

The back streets were all lined with evergreens and featured large, central parking lots covered in stone pavers. Around those lots were an array of small townhomes, each with area businesses and mom-and-pop-type stores. There were lawyers' offices adept at setting up financial planning for creatures that lived over two centuries, dry cleaners capable of removing grass, mud and blood stains, shoe repair stores that could custom make coverings for hooved feet, holistic medical clinics that specialized in shifters, and many other services for the community at large.

They were all respectable businesses and would happily take care of any patron that stepped foot on their premises, be they human or other. And while most humans were ignorant of the world around them, they were also happy to be in such a tight-knit community where everyone was welcome, and no one was a stranger.

Unless of course they *were* a stranger, and then they were scrutinized closely by supernatural and human alike. It had taken Torie saving the town from a dark threat on more than one occasion before everyone warmed to her and embraced her as a native.

And that was why Max was so unsettled by the body found behind the bus stop two streets back from main street. Even in broad daylight, no one had seen this young woman get off the bus, walk through the building, or purchase one of the daily Town Crier papers shoved in her backpack. She was propped up against the back of the building next to a door used by one of the two employees who worked for the transit system.

It was one of those employees, Alice Gibbs, who had stumbled upon the girl when she stepped outside to have a smoke. The poor woman had almost tripped over the body, and it appeared to have scared her so badly that she may have just given up smoking altogether, right there on the spot. She was sitting in an old, plastic chair on the opposite side of a dumpster as one of Max's deputies took her statement.

Max was standing next to the body, staring intently, when Torie, Jasmin, Fionna and Elric walked up. Someone had carefully laid a blue vinyl covering over it with the word CORONER written in yellow block print.

Max stood to greet his friends; his typically somber demeanor was even more depressed than usual.

"Max, you said this was something we needed to see," Torie said, placing a comforting hand on the big sheriff's shoulder.

He nodded and took a deep breath. "I wasn't sure what to make of this. It's not the typical M.O. for a normal death."

He reached down and drew back the cover, revealing the body of a young girl, probably in her very late teens, maybe twenty, with straight blonde hair that flowed down past her shoulders. She was dressed in jeans that were strategically ripped at the knees and upper thighs, a red tank top, and a blue jean jacket.

The reason for Max's concern was immediately apparent. The girl's eyes were missing. In their place, were blacked-out holes. It looked like she had applied smokey black makeup to the area around where her orbs had once been.

Other than that, there was nothing else to indicate how she might have died.

"No trauma to the body whatsoever," said Max. "No signs of a fight, nothing to indicate what could have done this."

Both Fionna and Elric leaned in closer, noses quivering.

"Yeah, I couldn't detect any scent on her either," Max responded.

"Not only is there no scent of anyone else on her, but *she* doesn't have a scent," said Elric.

"No…there's something there," said Fionna, closing her eyes and inhaling deeper. "It's very faint, but…I can't place it. She smells like old rocks."

"Rocks?" Max said, frowning. "I can't smell that."

"My nose is even more sensitive than a wolf's," she replied. "Most shifters that are prey animals usually are."

Max scribbled in his notebook as Torie and Jasmin leaned in to examine the body.

Jasmin held up both hands, touching the tips of her

thumbs and forefingers together to form a triangle, through which she peered.

"Nothing," she said. "There is no magical signature anywhere on the body."

Torie stood, looking around to make sure no one was watching, as her eyes began to glow blue.

"I call on spirits to lift any veil,
that may now cause our eyes to fail."

The whispered incantation caused the body to briefly glow, the faintest of blue light shimmering around the form. It was a brief flash, before dissipating entirely. Torie and Jasmin exchanged looks.

"Nothing," said Torie.

"Those burns around her eyes...what could have done that?" asked Elric. "There is no gun powder or explosive residue. I've never seen anything like this."

"There is also no residual smell in the air of anything inorganic, like wires or plastic burning," said Max.

"So, we can rule out lightning," said Jasmin. "Maybe it was spontaneous human combustion."

Torie's eyes widened. "Are you saying that's real? I was always told that was just something made up by the National Enquirer. You don't know how many sleepless nights I had because of that and quicksand."

Jasmin arched an eyebrow. "For me, it was the Bermuda triangle. I was convinced that at some point in my life I would be flying over it and just disappear."

Max cleared his throat. "It sounds like we are all in agreement that whatever caused this is not something known to man."

"Or woman," said Fionna, before catching the look everyone gave her. "What? I'm just saying."

"What we know is that this is not a normal death," said Jasmin. "It's definitely supernatural. We just need to figure out what did this."

"Any idea who she was?" asked Torie.

"We're running her face through the missing person's database right now, hoping for a hit," Max replied.

"Any chance she could be a member of the community? Many of the colleges are headed into their breaks next week, maybe she came home a couple days early?" asked Jasmin.

Max shook his head. "It's possible. We are working on that angle as well. But Alice Gibbs knows just about everyone in this town. She's never seen this girl before. And no one inside or outside saw her. We've spoken with the bus driver who pulled in most recently, and he swears she wasn't on the bus."

"So where did she come from?" said Torie, speaking more to herself than the others. "She glanced down at the girl's feet. "Those are Vasque hiking boots she's wearing. They're very well made and not cheap. Waterproof and... great for maintaining your footing around slippery rocks." She glanced at Fionna, nodding.

The squirrel shifter bent close, closing her eyes as she sniffed the boots. Then, she stood, walking around the perimeter of the bus station, staring closely at the ground before moving inside and walking through, doing the same thing.

She came back, shaking her head. "There's nothing. It's almost as if she didn't step foot anywhere near or in the station. Almost as if she was just dropped here out of thin air."

"This has magic written all over it," said Jasmin. "We just need to figure out how."

"And why," added Torie. "I'm assuming she wasn't carrying anything in her bag that stood out; other than that paper, I mean."

Max looked at her, blinking.

"You did check her for ID, didn't you...?" Torie said.

The big werewolf huffed. "I mean, I wasn't the first one on the scene..."

He bent and began rummaging through her bag. Aside from the paper, there were a couple of tubes of lipstick, a hairbrush, compact, bottled water, a couple of health bars, and her wallet. He glanced at Torie, then opened the wallet, searching through it. There was a large amount of cash inside, but no ID of any kind.

"Well, we know that this was deliberate," said Jasmin. "Why else would someone have taken anything to identify her and left all of that money?"

Max unzipped the back pocket of the backpack and reached inside, fishing around. He pulled out a delicate, gold necklace, with a tiny medallion dangling from it.

Jasmin's eyes lit up. "Give that to us. Jewelry can be great transmitters of a person's aura. We might be able to use it to find out more about her."

Torie could see the hesitation on Max's face. This wasn't the first time they had asked him to break the chain of custody, but she also knew he understood the reasoning behind it. While there were a fair number of shifters that made up his force, there were still human political figures he answered to who had no idea how things sometimes had to work in Singing Falls.

He glanced around, then quickly slid the necklace into Jasmin's hand.

"We'll keep this quiet and get it back to you when we can," Torie said. He mumbled in response.

They watched as a black sedan pulled up and the medical examiner climbed out, waving at them as he approached.

It had taken some time and a good bit of searching, but the town had finally secured a supernatural to fill the job of medical examiner. Singing Falls had gone through a number of professionals in that position. Most humans didn't last in the role. Their minds weren't built for accepting things that couldn't always be explained by science and medicine.

Dr. Emil Faun was a sprite, an offshoot of the fae, and he had moved to Singing Falls to become the chief medical examiner for the county. It had not taken long for him to make Singing Falls his home, and the community had embraced him with open arms. While not a practitioner of green magic himself, his knowledge of the subject and the supernatural beings that made up Singing Falls was second to none.

He waved, giving a quick tilt backwards in greeting. His ever-present slight smile widened when he saw Jasmin.

"Hello, ladies," he said. It was an acknowledgement of all of them, but Torie couldn't help but feel like it was directed at Jasmin alone. "Max, Elric; what have we got?"

Max stepped aside so he could get a view of the body.

"Interesting," said the doctor, pulling out a pair of nitrile exam gloves from his pocket and snapping them on. He bent close, placing the tip of his forefinger on her chin to slightly move her head from one side to the other.

"Ever see anything like this before, Doc?" Max asked.

The examiner didn't look up from his work, mumbling his response. "No."

He opened a small, leather case he carried with him and withdrew a tiny green vial with a glass stopper. Reaching over, he held his hand over the body, then closed his hand tightly into a fist before snapping it open quickly. A red mist rose from the body, and he quickly waved his hand through it, directing the mist into the vial. Once stoppered, he placed the vial with the mist in it back into his bag, before leaning in closer, placing his ear on the dead girl's chest.

"Um, I'm pretty sure she's dead," said Max, folding his arms across his chest.

The medical examiner lifted his head, took out a tiny notebook and scribbled in it. "That wasn't what I was listening for." He stood, carefully taking off his gloves. "Life echoes. Sometimes, in the newly departed, the body can tell us a lot about what they went through in their last moments."

Jasmin's eyes lit up. "I've never heard that before. Is it something that can be detected mystically, or are your senses especially attuned to it?"

Dr. Faun gave a slight smile, his eyes sparkling. "For me, it's something I can pick up with my hearing. However, it is something witches can be taught to ferret out as well. If you know what to look for that is."

Jasmin returned his smile before quickly looking away.

"I mean…I can teach you, if you're interested," he said, then quickly looked at Torie, a slight blush to his cheeks. "Both of you. I can teach you both. If you like."

Torie smiled, making mental note.

"Ah, one last thing," the medical examiner said. He reached into his bag and withdrew a cotton swab. Bending forward, he carefully swabbed the burn areas around where the girl's eyes had been. Then, almost reverentially, he placed the swab in a plastic tube, took out another tiny vial, and squeezed a few drops of liquid into the tube with the swab, before replacing everything back into his bag. "That should be all I need to preserve until I can examine the body closer in my lab."

"Do you have any guess as to what happened to her?" asked Max.

The doctor shook his head. "I don't deal in guesses."

"Well, have you seen anything like this before?" Torie asked.

He considered her question for a moment before answering. "Twice. Once was from an energy vampire; the second was a case of spontaneous human combustion." He turned to head back to his car before raising a forefinger and facing the group of friends. "Speaking of, did you know that among all living creatures, spontaneous combustion is unique to only the human race? Fascinating."

And with that, he was off, humming lightly to himself as he headed back to his car, stopping only to give directions to the drivers of the paramedic unit that would transport the body for him.

"See!" said Fionna, "It is real!"

Torie rolled her eyes. "I can guarantee that wasn't what killed her." She turned, heading back to her own car. "Time to examine this necklace. Maybe, between that and whatever Faun finds, we can narrow down what happened to her. Oh, Max…can you come over, please?"

The werewolf gave her a steely glance. "I'm kinda busy here, Torie. The paperwork on this will take me most of the night."

"It's important. I've thought of a new appetizer that's made with fillet mignon and red wine. I need your refined palate."

He blinked repeatedly, staring at her. "I'll be there in two hours."

She smiled, clapping her hands. "Perfect."

Before she could say anything else, her phone pinged. She took it out, flicking at the screen before frowning at what she was seeing.

"Torie? What is it?" asked Jasmin.

"It's Shawn. He's here for a visit." She looked up at her friends. "He's at the house."

Jasmin's eyes grew wide. "You mean the house we just enchanted to clean itself?"

Fionna clasped her hands over her mouth. "And the one with a dragon prowling around acting as guard dog?"

Torie caught her breath. "No time for the car. Elric, meet me at the house." She tossed her boyfriend the keys before joining hands with Jasmin.

The two witches closed their eyes and whispered an incantation that whisked the two of them and Fionna away in a cloud of sparkles.

Standing behind, Elric frowned, clenching his jaw as he stared at the spot where the woman he loved had been standing.

Chapter Three

The three women appeared on the immaculate lawn, just off the large stone patio of Torie's house.

"Fionna, find Leo and put him in the study," Torie said as she and Jasmin headed for the large French doors that led into the kitchen.

In a flash, Fionna shifted into her squirrel form and scampered up the side of the house, and onto the upper terrace off the master bedroom. Within seconds she had disappeared into the house.

Entering the kitchen, Torie took a quick look around, making sure everything was where it should be, and nothing was moving around of its own magical accord. Jasmin raised her hands, bending her fingers into the form of a cross as she began to cast a spell.

"No!" Torie said, spinning to stop her just as her son walked into the kitchen, a single duffel bag hanging from one shoulder.

"Mom?" he said, peering across the island.

"Shawn, baby!" Torie said, skipping across the floor to

scoop her only son into her arms. "What...what are you doing here? And how did you get in?"

"The door was open," he replied in whispered tones as her hug forced the air from his lungs. "You shouldn't leave your door unlocked like that."

"Oh...I wasn't thinking. We were just out back, straightening up the, um, storage building. Right, Jasmin?"

"Oh, yep, that's what we were doing alright. Didn't hear you ringing the doorbell," Jasmin added.

"I didn't see your car in the drive, so that was when I texted you," he said. "Where's your car?"

"Oh, that? It's...being detailed. Yes, Elric has it. You remember him, right?"

Shawn rolled his eyes. "Yes, Mom, I remember your boyfriend."

There was a thump that came from somewhere outside of the room, followed by a few quick footsteps.

"What was that?" Shawn asked. "Is someone else upstairs?"

"That's just our friend Fionna. She's helping too. With stuff in the storage. But had to...get something from the study upstairs," Torie replied. She could see Shawn's brow furrow and quickly tried to change the subject. "Where's your car? How did you get here?"

"I took a Lyft from the airport. You know I'm not fond of driving and I certainly wasn't about to tackle these winding mountain roads to get up here."

Now it was Torie who frowned. "Why didn't you tell me you were coming? I would have picked you up. That's a long drive from the airport to Singing Falls."

Shawn waved her off. "Oh no, it wasn't bad. Gave me plenty of time to admire the beauty of this place. It's really stunning. And I wanted to surprise you."

She hugged him again. "Well, you certainly did that."

Shawn held his mother at arm's length, looking questionably into her eyes.

"Mom, is something wrong? Is it not a good time for me to be here?"

"What? Absolutely it is a good time. You are welcome here anytime you want."

"Good. Because there is something I need to talk to you about. Just not right now." He looked away, not meeting her eyes before she could question him further. "But this place is amazing. You've done an incredible job."

She smiled, appreciating the compliment.

Just then, there was more slamming coming from upstairs, followed by a rush of footsteps coming down the stairs.

"Oh, no you don't!" exclaimed Fionna. "You come back here."

Just then, Leo burst into the kitchen. Torie's eyes grew wide just as Shawn was turning to see what all the commotion was about. His eyes locked on Leo, at the same time as Torie and Jasmin. Yet instead of a baby dragon, there was a marbled cat, sitting there licking its paws before coming over to nuzzle up against Torie.

"Mom, I didn't know you had a cat. I thought you were allergic."

Torie exchanged glances with Jasmin. "No, honey, I must have grown out of that. But I wasn't sure if you were, so that was why Fionna was trying to get him into his carrier upstairs. You remember my friend, Fionna, right?"

She gave a small nod to the squirrel shifter who smiled at Shawn, her eyes darting back and forth between him and Leo.

"Oh sure, nice to see you again," Shawn said. He picked

up his bag and turned to Torie. "Do you mind if I drop this somewhere? I could also use a shower…"

His voice trailed off as his eyes focused on something over Torie's shoulder.

She turned, following his eyes out the French doors to the back of the house. Elric was coming out of the pool house, shirtless and fastening a pair of pants.

"Does he ever wear clothes?" Shawn asked. "No. Never mind. I don't want to hear the answer to that."

"Here, why don't you come with me. I'll show you to any number of the guest rooms upstairs and you can have your pick," said Fionna, taking him by the arm and leading him out of the kitchen.

Torie could hear her making small talk to distract him as she made her way to the back door, opening it for Elric.

"Where did you come from? Where's my car?" she asked.

"I needed to burn off some energy, so I ran here. Max is bringing your car later."

Torie frowned. "You didn't set off any of the wards protecting the place."

The house was built on a ridge and the back had been leveled by a retaining wall with a high, iron fence jutting upward from the stone. Beyond the wall was a thirty-foot drop down the side of the ridge, leading to the wilderness beyond.

"Well, your wards aren't designed to stop anyone you know from entering," said Jasmin. "And I'm impressed, Elric, with the jump you would have had to make to get over the fence from the ground."

He smiled, bowing slightly at the witch.

"Still," said Torie, "I should have felt something when you entered. For that matter, why didn't I sense Shawn entering the house until it was almost too late? He nearly caught you using magic."

"We'll figure that out later. What I want to know is how did you cast that glamour over Leo so quickly? Even I didn't feel a hint of magic when you did it."

Torie shook her head in dismay. "I was about to ask you the same thing. I didn't do it."

Jasmin frowned, looking at the dragon that now looked exactly like a cat. "Well, if you didn't do it, and I didn't do it; who did?"

"Maybe he did it himself," said Elric, moving to the refrigerator and rummaging through. "He's a dragon after all. Who knows what they are capable of."

Jasmin and Torie stared at one another before looking once again at Leo.

"No way," said Jasmin. "He's not a shifter. Something else is at play here."

"Well, whatever it is, we don't have time for it right now. Hopefully, he stays like that until Shawn leaves. Speaking of which, he seems…I don't know…distracted."

There was a clatter as Elric dropped a platter of meatballs on the floor. The pantry door flew open and a broom, followed by a sponge mop, floated out, heading for the mess. At the same time, Leo shot forward, making a beeline for the spilt food.

"Oh, no you don't," said Torie, waving an arm in the air and scooping up the little dragon in a glowing bubble before pulling him back to her arms. "The last time you ate cooked food your stomach was a mess."

Jasmin swept her arm into the air as well, sending the broom and mop back into the pantry, much to Elric's dismay.

"Fine, I'll clean it up myself," he grumbled, sitting the

rest of the plates onto the island and reaching for the roll of paper towels.

"Should we remove the enchantments here in the kitchen?" Torie asked. "At least until Shawn is gone."

Jasmin pursed her lips, deep in thought. "It took us a while to get these just right. If we undo them, who knows what effect that could have. We might not be able to recast a spell just like this a second time."

"It's kind of creepy," said Elric, as he was bent over cleaning up the food. "I mean, don't get me wrong, it definitely comes in handy, but also——" he stood, moving to throw the paper towels away, "——very creepy to see."

"Must be a shifter thing," said Jasmin, "Cos I plan to do the same all over my house once we work the bugs out here."

"Wait, you're still working the bugs out?" It was Fionna who had made her way back into the kitchen.

Jasmin waved her off. "It's fine. Magic stuff, and all that. We'll get it all worked out in time. But right now, we have more pressing matters. Like a dead body that we still don't know anything about."

Torie's eyes widened. "The necklace."

Jasmin nodded. "We need to cast a spell, see what it can tell us. But not with Shawn in the house. We could do it at my place."

Torie snapped her finger. "Or we send him out for a bit while we do what we need to." She looked imploringly at Elric, giving him a wry smile.

"What?" said the werewolf.

"Well, I want to have a nice dinner for Shawn tonight. But I don't have enough steaks. Why don't you take him to the market when he's done showering, maybe kill some time. Get everything we need for dinner tonight. Then, we invite Max over and make an evening of it." She turned to Fionna. "And you invite Glen. It's been too long since we all had a big sit down. Jasmin and I will work on the necklace and try to calm down the magical kitchen a bit."

"I…I mean, sure," stammered Elric. "I guess. I just…I don't know what to talk to a human teenager about."

"He's nineteen," Torie said. "Talk to him about whatever you would talk to Max about. No, on second thought, take your cues from him. It will be a good chance for you to get to know one another."

He sighed and bent down to give her a kiss. She playfully smacked him on the backside and told him to go through the fridge and start making a list of everything they needed.

"What can we bring?" asked Fionna.

"I'll have everything. Why don't you bring the dessert? I won't have time to make that," Torie replied.

Fionna nodded and turned to leave. "Want me to take Leo? You and Jasmin are going to be busy. At least this way, I can entertain him for a bit. I'll bring him back tonight."

"Sure. Thank you," Torie said. She turned to Jasmin. "Ready?"

"As ready as I can be. I think this is something we can do downstairs in the nexus room. Might as well try it out."

Elric frowned. "More magical rooms?"

"Something like that," Torie said with a smile. "Have fun with Shawn. Tell him I'm planning things for later and will talk with him soon." She went to follow Jasmin out of the kitchen but then turned towards Elric one last time. "And don't sniff him. You'll just freak him out doing that."

Elric rolled his eyes playfully and set about writing his shopping list as the women exited the room.

They reached the door to Torie's basement, and just as

she reached for the knob, the door swung open of its own accord.

Torie frowned, looking back over her shoulder at Jasmin. "Did you do that?"

"No. Wasn't me."

"Great. So now, on top of a supernatural murder and a surprise visit from my son, we now have ghosts."

Chapter Four

The basement of Torie's house consisted of an entertainment area complete with wet bar, massive television paired with a state-of-the-art sound system, a dry sauna, workout area, and a wine cellar. There was also a room behind the entertainment area that could only be accessed by a single, warded door. It was designed to be at the very center of the house in order to absorb and focus magical energies that flowed through the ley lines flowing through the earth.

Aside from Torie's personal study and her kitchen, this was her most favorite room in the house. The walls were roughhewn stone that kept the room a perfect temperature. The ceiling was covered in a warm, golden-toned stucco that reminded her of the burning hues of a setting sun. She had eschewed can lights in favor of a spectacular hanging ball light that was made of black iron and amber bulbs. Sconces along the wall cast their light upward, adding to the serene ambiance.

The room was sparsely furnished with only a large, comfortable sofa, a reading chair, and a round, crafted wooden table in the center of the space. The base of the table was an ornately carved dragon holding up the top. It was a nod to Leo, and she loved the piece of furniture almost as much as she did the little dragon himself.

Jasmin joined her at the table, standing on the opposite side from her friend. Torie took the necklace from the small bag in which she carried it and laid it on the table just as there was a slight dimming of the lights before they returned to full brightness.

"If this is a ghost, we need to deal with it," Torie said.

"It's not a ghost. They only flicker lights in movies. This is probably something with your electrical. Once this is all over, I suggest getting it checked out."

"What about the door opening on its own?"

"I don't know what that was, but I'm still saying it wasn't a ghost. Ghosts can't move physical objects in the human world. Even your mother couldn't do that."

Torie nodded slowly, her mind drifting back to the specter of her mother. Not a day went by that she didn't miss her, and part of her hoped to see the woman again someday. Jasmin saw the look of longing on her face and her eyes softened.

"It's not her, Torie."

"You're right. My mother has moved on, and I know that. Still…you have to admit, something weird is going on here."

Jasmin sighed. "It's Singing Falls. There is always something weird going on. Now, how much time do we have? We need to get started on this."

Torie frowned but nodded. Jasmin was right. Since

moving to Singing Falls, Torie had encountered more than her fair share of the strange and unexplained. Granted, most of those things had tried to kill her at some point, but that didn't mean she had grown to respect the variety of weirdness that proliferated in the town. She wasn't keen on the thought that something might have taken up residence in her house, but whatever it was, she had faith in her and Jasmin's abilities to deal with it later.

But right now, they had to focus on the task at hand.

The necklace chain was very thin and fragile. To the point that Torie had to handle it with the utmost care for fear of it breaking. A round medallion with a quarter-moon sliver embossed on it sparkled in the low light, drawing their attention. Turning it over revealed no clues as to its owner, no embossing or engraved initials anywhere.

Placing it on the table, Torie held one hand over it, invoking a cleansing spell designed to remove the influence of anyone who touched it other than its rightful owner.

"Wait," said Jasmin. She held out her hands and cast a shimmering blue bubble around them and the table. "Just in case there is something going on with the magic in this house. We don't need any unwanted interference."

"Good idea," said Torie.

Once they were both convinced there was no way any magic could leak out or in, they cast their gaze onto the necklace and began to chant.

> *"We call on spirits that have no name,*
> *to reveal to us from whence this came."*

At first nothing happened, and the witches looked on in confusion. The spell was spoken, the intent was focused; but there was no revelation.

"Are you concentrating?" asked Jasmin.

"Of course I am. Something must have gone——"

A flash of light silenced the witches. It bloomed outward, causing them to shield their eyes behind a raised forearm.

"What in the world?" Torie reached out with her mind, touching Jasmin's shields, letting out a mental sigh of relief that they were still intact.

Following the light, a wind swept through the enclosed space. They were in a vacuum, so it shouldn't have been possible, but Torie felt her hair whipping about as she was once again forced to protect her eyes.

Then, as if wind existing where there should be none wasn't surprising enough, the wind began to speak.

It was more like a garbled moan; hot air being squeezed through bellows that the witches realized were words.

"Who..." came the harshness, "dares..."

Torie looked at Jasmin. Neither of them responded, but each gathered their magic, focusing it into their fists in the form of glowing circles, ready to be unleashed at a moment's notice if needed.

The air swirled and died down before rising again. The pendant floated into the air above the table, rotating until the medallion faced them.

"Yesss," it hissed, "I see youuuu."

"Okay, enough of that," said Jasmin. She held both hands in front of her, twisted them until one was above the other, palms facing, then slammed them together. The spell she and Torie had cast was broken and the wind died down instantly while the pendant dropped back to the table.

"What the heck was that?" demanded Torie.

Jasmin was staring at the necklace. "Not sure. But...did you get a sense of malevolence from it?"

Torie thought about what she said, searching her feelings as she shook her head. "No, I didn't. Not exactly, I mean. I sensed great power and anger; but no ill will."

Jasmin was nodding. "Same here. Whatever that was, it seemed surprised, but not aggressive."

"I didn't like that it said it could see us. Good work shutting that down so quickly."

"Hopefully, the good doctor will learn something from examining the body of that girl; because we got nothing." She scooped the necklace up and handed it to Torie. "I think you better seal this away in one of those special lock boxes in your study."

She meant the small containment caskets that had once been used against them by a chimera. They had housed the organs of some of the most powerful shifters in the world and had all but been destroyed in the battle against two powerful witches determined to kill Torie.

"Good idea," she replied. "But we did learn something. Whatever that thing was, it couldn't have had anything to do with that poor dead girl."

"Not necessarily," said Jasmin as they left the room. "We asked to learn about the owner of the necklace. Who's to say what we conjured wasn't the original owner?"

It wasn't something Torie had considered, but she knew that Jasmin was right. If the necklace didn't belong to the girl, then where had she acquired something with this kind of power attached to it?

The house was eerily quiet as the two women entered the main floor. This was one of the few times since its construction that Torie had found it empty. Despite its immense size, having Elric and her friends, as well as a full-time dragon romping around inside, made it feel almost cozy.

"I need to go get changed, then I'll head back over to help set up for this evening," Jasmin said. She gave Torie a goodbye hug, then pointed at the necklace. "Don't forget, lock that up. Last thing we need is it interacting with your… ghost, for lack of a better word."

She turned to leave, and Torie called after her, "You said it wasn't a ghost!"

Jasmin waved without turning around and was out the door. She headed for the path leading to her house, and once again, Torie was grateful for the fact that her best friend lived right next door. There was always comfort in knowing reinforcements lived so close by, just in case.

Her personal study was located at the rear of the house and was a combination of an office and home library. Unlike the larger, more public space she had designed on the upper level, this one was filled with knick-knacks of a more magical nature, as well as a plethora of spell books, and rare objects de art that had belonged to her mother.

The furnishings in the room were simple; a large desk, one wall of floor-to-ceiling bookcases, a couple of wingback chairs arranged around the fireplace, a few tables and a comfortable cloth ottoman that acted as a footrest and a coffee table.

When she entered the space, the automatic lighting system came to life, flooding the room with soft light from lamps arranged near the seating areas and on the desk. With a thought, she brought the fireplace to life. Though it wasn't particularly cold, and the house had exceptional insulation, she loved the unmatched ambience of a wood-burning fireplace. There was just nothing like it to settle her nerves.

The containment boxes that weren't destroyed sat on one of the bookshelves next to a collection of crystals and a large, jade gemstone Torie had found in her mother's possessions after she passed away.

Well, after the second and final time she passed away.

Torie eyed the three boxes on the shelf and finally selected one that was pewter-colored, with emerald-green stones inlaid in an intricate pattern across the top. Removing the box, she set it on the desk, carefully opening the top to reveal an interior of dark green, satin cloth. Holding one hand over the container, she felt for the spells that had been placed around the box to seal anything placed within.

Satisfied everything was as it should be, she placed the necklace inside, closed it, and whispered an added layer of protection as she placed it back on the shelf. Just as she was turning to leave, she noticed one of the leather-bound books on the shelf move slightly of its own accord. Torie stared, thinking that maybe her eyes were playing tricks. But no, she was meticulous about keeping all her book spines in a tight, smooth row. One of them was definitely jutting out farther than the others.

Walking over to it, she pulled the odd one out, realizing it was a book of spells that she had been meaning to read for some time. It was more of a handwritten journal than a book; one of her mother's personal tomes that had been hidden behind a fake wall at her old house.

She ran her hand lightly over the front cover, tracing the embossed designs with her fingertips. She stopped moving. This was her mother's spell book.

Her mother's.

"Mom? Are you there? Is this you trying to reach out to me?"

Nothing happened, and she thought she was beginning to let her wishful thinking get the better of her. She remembered what Jasmin said about ghosts not being able to touch the physical world, despite what Hollywood loved to depict in horror movies.

But maybe that was only the case with mortal ghosts? What if the ghost was a deceased witch? And a powerful one at that. Almost all supernaturals operated under a different set of rules to humans. Why should this one be any different?

She stood there, sending her senses outward, feeling for any sign of magical energy in the room, any ripple of the supernatural.

Nothing.

She was about to dismiss the entire event, when the orange and gray throw blanket draped over one of the wingback chairs lifted and flung itself into her arms. Shock rooted her to the spot as she held the blanket.

Slowly, she brought it to her nose and was nearly overcome with emotion as the scent of her mother assaulted her memories. She choked back tears.

"Mom, it is you."

She held the blanket close, waiting for more signs that didn't come. But that was alright. Her mother had returned to her once before, cheating death. And now it had happened again.

She left the room content and focused.

Jasmin would tell her what she was considering was not something she should ever consider; it bordered on black magic. But Torie knew what she had to do.

It was time to raise the dead. But first, she had a dinner party to plan.

She smiled as she exited her office. She headed down the stairs, her mind filled with recipes and potential spells for what she needed to do.

And she never noticed the door to her office slowly begin to close, the latch locking itself from the inside with a satisfying little click.

Chapter Five

Elric and Shawn made it back to the house just as Torie had finished her shower and was setting out a selection of wine and whiskeys in the kitchen bar area. She selected a bold red that would complement the grilled steaks, and whiskey for those guests who might want something a little harder, but also smoother, than a Cabernet.

She was in the midst of grinding some black peppercorns when their laughter flitted through the house as they made their way through the mudroom from the garage. In a matter of minutes, the large island was almost covered in reusable cloth bags overflowing with goods.

"Okay, you didn't have to buy out the store," she joked, looking at the haul.

"They had just unloaded a shipment of fresh vegetables from the local farms," Elric said. "And the butcher was very good at selling us on the latest cuts of beef and pork." He leaned in to give her a quick peck on the lips.

"Oh please, you were looking for a reason to buy out the meat counter," said Shawn, trying to stifle a laugh. "That poor man barely got a word out and you were like, 'yes, I'll take one of everything'."

Elric laughed in return. "Well, what about you, mister 'do you have any plant-based goods, and were all of these animals free range and grass fed'? The look on the man's face when all he could say was…"

The two of them finished his sentence in unison. "All I can say is they all died happy."

They each burst out laughing, one using the other to steady themself as they bent over, holding their stomach at the memory.

"Well, that sounds terrible," Torie said.

"What do you mean?" asked Shawn.

"I mean, I now hate the thought of eating animals that were so happy when they met their end."

Elric and Shawn looked at one another before bursting out in laughter yet again.

Despite herself, Torie laughed with the two of them. Whatever fears she had about them getting along seemed to have been quelled.

"Well, the least you can do is unpack all that meat and put it in the freezer in the pantry. I'm going to start prepping the vegetables and the sauce for the steaks. I'll be ready for one of you to light the grill soon."

"On it," said Elric, sweeping up four large bags and heading for the pantry.

"Show off," called Shawn after him.

Then, he eased up to his mother's side and leaned his weight against her.

She smiled as she began to finely dice an onion. "What's going on, Shawn? You good?"

He sighed and nodded. "I really like Elric. I can see

what you see in him. Well, mostly. He still needs to wear more clothes."

Now it was Torie who couldn't help but laugh. She leaned her head against her son, the way they used to before.

Before he had left for college. Before his father had left her for another woman and cost them everything. Before she had become a witch.

It seemed like a lifetime ago, but here, in her kitchen, with the smell of vegetables fresh from a garden, and his easy-going laughter filling the room, everything came rushing back to her as if it were only yesterday.

"Mom. I really need to talk to you when we get a chance."

She turned to face her only son and saw that he couldn't meet her eyes.

"What is it? You know you can tell me anything."

Before he could attempt a response, they were interrupted by Jasmin as she walked into the kitchen.

"Look who I found outside," she said. Fionna, holding hands with her wife Glen, trailed in after her. She was carrying a large box with an open top covered in plastic wrap. Glen carried Leo the cat in her arms, and Torie gave him a hard long look, thankful that whatever glam had been cast over him was still holding.

Fionna set the large box down on the center island, letting everyone admire the mountain of petit fours and cheesecake bites in various flavors. Removing the wrap released an aroma of sugars and vanilla that made Fionna do a little happy dance to everyone's amusement.

Torie took her son by the hand. "Come on. Let's go to my study and chat."

Shawn smiled and politely pulled away. "Later. Right now, I want you to focus on all this."

Torie hesitated but also knew that whatever it was her son wanted to talk about, now wasn't the right time. She watched him sidle up to Fionna, laughing at something she couldn't hear. She couldn't help but smile at the squirrel shifter playfully. Looking around, she didn't see Leo and hoped he had made his way to the back of the house and his favorite spot; the cushions that had been arranged under Torie's desk in her study.

"What can I do?" asked Glen, stepping up to stand next to Torie.

Torie looked around and pointed. "How about you start setting out the place settings. It's a beautiful evening, so I say we dine under the stars."

"You got it," Glen replied as she began to pick up the plates to cart outdoors.

Jasmin walked slowly past her, finger slowly jabbing in the air as she counted in a light whisper.

"You have one set too many," she said to Torie.

Torie smiled and gave her friend a wink. "You never know when someone might drop in."

Jasmin frowned. "What does that mean?"

Torie shrugged and changed the subject. "Something happened after you left."

Jasmin arched a single eyebrow. "Did your ghost visit again?"

"In a manner of speaking." Torie looked around, making sure no one was in ear shot. "Jasmin, I think it's my mother. I think she's back. Again."

Jasmin was perfectly still as she stared at her friend. "Are you sure?"

That wasn't the response Torie had expected. She fully

expected her friend to scoff at her and explain all the reasons why that couldn't be the case. She was half *hoping* for that to have been the response.

"Well, no, I'm not one hundred percent...but, I just have a feeling. I think she is trying to let me know that she maybe needs help reaching through to me; maybe she is stuck somewhere." She reached into one of the island drawers and removed two large grill grates for the vegetables. "I mean, I was expecting you to tell me I was crazy; that ghosts couldn't do the things we experienced earlier."

The drawer to the island closed quietly on its own, and the two witches stared at one another.

"Okay, that was just the kitchen magic doing its thing," Jasmin said. "Just a coincidence it happened as we mentioned your mother."

"I thought you said there was no such thing as coincidence."

"Yeah, well, I also said that ghosts can't move physical objects around and look how that's turning out." She stopped, taking a deep breath and holding it, before slowly exhaling. "Look, there are things that I think I know. But lately, since meeting you, a lot has changed. I trust your instincts. Enough to at least look at this closer when we get the chance."

"If it is my mother though, it couldn't be worse timing."

"What? Your mother's back?"

Both women jumped, spinning around to see Fionna standing right behind them.

"Girl, don't do that," said Jasmin. "And mind your business."

Fionna ignored her, eyes locking on Torie. "Is she back again? Is she haunting this house now? That would be cool.

Maybe she was the one who changed Leo to a cat so he wouldn't scare Shawn."

Torie started to answer, but Jasmin waved her off, a startled look on her face.

"What?" asked Torie.

"You, dear Fionna, are brilliant. Tell me, when you took Leo to your house, did his appearance revert to a dragon, or did he stay a cat?"

Fionna frowned. "Now that you mention it, he stayed a cat."

Jasmin was nodding. "You just asked if Torie's mom was haunting 'this house' now. Well, ghosts are attached to the place they died. She couldn't manifest here. Unless she were attached to something else. Something Torie could have brought here that was very important to her."

"That could be almost anything in my office," Torie said.

"True. But let's just say that she was responsible for casting a glamour spell on Leo. There is no way it would have held up while he was at Fionna's. The spell would have been broken. I think there is something else at work here, Torie. I'm sorry."

"Like you said, we will figure it out. It's not like there isn't enough going on around here." She reached for the grill basket and accidentally knocked over the pepper mill, spilling a few black grains across the quartz top.

Instantly, a couple of paper towels tore themselves free from the roll and floated towards her. She quickly snatched them out of the air, making sure no one saw.

"And this is why we are eating outside tonight," she added.

Max arrived, just as everything was prepped and ready for the grill.

"I left your keys in that weird bowl on the table in the entry," he said. "Tell your boyfriend he owes me a lift back to my place tonight."

He plopped down at the island, squinting at Torie.

"What's going on? Why are you so stressed?"

"I'm not stressed. No more so than usual," she replied.

He smirked. "I can smell your stress levels. They are way high."

Her eyes blazed as she wheeled on him. "Honestly, if one more supernatural tells me how I smell I'm going to ——" She stopped mid-threat as Shawn walked in, picking up the last of the food items to take out to the grill.

"Hi, honey," she said cheerfully, "This is Max. I don't think you've met him. He's the town sheriff and a friend of Elric's."

Max extended a hand, shaking the young man's firmly. "Nice to meet you, Shawn. I've heard a lot about you."

Shawn frowned slightly, glancing at his mother. "Nice to meet you as well."

He picked up a large, wooden butcher block cutting board, laid a few grilling accessories across it, and headed back out of the house.

Torie waited to make sure he was out of earshot before turning back to Max.

"Were you able to find anything out about the girl's identity?"

Max shook his head as he made his way to the refrigerator, securing a beer. Popping the top with his thumb, he took a long drink from the bottle.

"Not yet. We're running her face through the missing persons database, but so far, no hits. No dental records, and her fingerprints aren't in the system. We have reached out to area colleges as well, but with the break starting, there isn't much hope we are going to find out who she is that way. At least not anytime soon."

"Have you heard from the medical examiner?"

Again, he shook his head. "Faun is good. Very thorough, and he works fast. We'll hear something sooner rather than later I'm betting." He stared at something just over her shoulder, tilting his head back slightly. "What's that about?"

She turned her head, following his gaze. Elric and Jasmin were on the patio, standing to one side away from the others. Elric's body was stiff, and he leaned in awkwardly, his arms bent at the elbows as he spoke, his hands animated by his words. Jasmin had her arms across her body, leaning in slightly, a scowl on her face.

Torie knew her friend well enough to know when she was hearing something she wasn't comfortable with.

"No idea," she mumbled, wiping her hands on the blue and yellow apron she wore.

"Want me to listen in?" Max offered.

She snapped her head around at the wolf. "Absolutely not!"

He shrugged, returning to his beer. He stopped, putting the bottle down mid-swig as he sniffed the air.

"Max, I swear, if you are smelling me…" Torie said, her eyes taking on an eerie orange glow.

He held up a hand, turning away from her. "No, not you. But why does your house suddenly smell like…magic. A lot of it." His voice trailed off as he took a couple of steps towards the entrance of the kitchen, then stopped. "It's gone. There was a sudden blooming of magic in here, then it just faded away. Weird."

"Oh that. Jasmin and I enchanted the kitchen to become self-cleaning."

"You what?"

She wasn't sure if his tone was one of disbelief or disapproval. Thankfully, she didn't have to ask for clarification as the doorbell rang. Max left to answer it, returning with Dr. Faun in tow.

"Speak of the devil, and he shall appear," the wolf said playfully.

"Emil," said Torie, shaking the doctor's hand. "I'm so glad you could make it."

The sprite offered a dazzling smile in return, then turned to Max.

"I most assuredly am no devil, but it's interesting that you mention that. Because I think one may have killed that young girl from earlier today."

Torie's mouth dropped open, but rather than explain, the doctor brushed past her, his eyes locked on something outside.

"Oh! I think I should probably go say hello to Jasmin," he stammered, leaving Torie and Max to stare questioningly at one another.

Chapter Six

Torie followed him, tongs in hand, catching up to the sprite just as he reached Elric and Jasmin. The two stopped their conversation immediately as he approached, Max and Torie trailing close behind.

"Jasmin," he said, eyes sparkling. "It's so good to see you again."

"Dr. Faun," she said, caught a little off guard. "I didn't know you were going to be here."

"Please, it's Emil. And I was quite happy to receive Torie's invitation. How could I say no?"

Torie blushed slightly at the look Jasmin gave her. "See. You never know when that extra place setting will be needed."

Jasmin leaned in, a smile masking her words. "You could have at least given me a heads up so I could have worn a better dress." She then whipped around, blasting the medical examiner with a megawatt smile and asked if he found the house alright.

"Oh yes. The navigation app was right on. How in the

world did we ever find anything without them? Navigating by the position of the stars just wasn't as efficient."

Both Jasmin and Torie blinked at the man, eyebrows raised.

"Alrighty then," said Torie, motioning for them to join her at the grill. "Why don't you tell us what you found?"

As they crowded around the grill, Torie placed the baskets of chopped vegetables on one side and then increased the heat on the other as she withdrew a plate of steaks that had been resting at room temperature. Just then, Leo walked through the crowd, arching his back and rubbing himself against Torie's legs.

"Not now," she said, gently. "I promise I'll save the best piece for you for later."

She looked up to see Dr. Faun staring intently at Leo the cat.

"Is that…what I think it is?" he asked, bending down to inspect Leo.

"Wait, you don't see a cat?" asked Jasmin.

"Of course not. That's a dragon. Dragonis Komodis… blue-winged, no doubt. Very rare. Where on earth did you get one?"

Torie took in a deep breath. "You know about dragons? You know what he is! You have to tell me everything."

Jasmin cleared her throat. "Maybe that can be saved for after whatever it is you're making us crowd around this hot grill to hear."

Torie looked at the doctor and nodded. "Tell them what you were just telling Max and me."

The doctor cleared his throat, tearing his eyes away from Jasmin as he addressed them all. "The girl, or rather young woman, as I can say with confidence that she was twenty-two years old, died as a result of a brain hemorrhage from the sudden heating of the blood vessels around her eyes to the point of bursting."

"As in...combustion?" questioned Fionna.

"Almost, but it was localized only to the eyes. Oh, and it came from an outside source."

"So definitely murder," said Max.

"Absolutely," replied the doctor. "There were trace amounts of brimstone found deep within her tissue. That was the accelerant that superheated her blood enough to..." He paused, then held up both fists near his head and suddenly spread all ten fingers.

Torie shivered at the graphic mental image she was forming. "And you think this was the work of some kind of...devil?"

"Hold up," said Jasmin. "The devil isn't real."

"Yeah, for once, I agree with Jasmin," said Elric.

"What are you talking about? When have you ever *not* agreed with me?" Jasmin replied.

Torie gave them a glance; the two were definitely acting weird. Something was off, but she didn't have time to worry about that. The steaks were calling out for attention and the last thing she wanted was to burn them. She used her tongs and gently flipped them as Emil continued the conversation.

"I did not say it was *the* devil; not the one you think of. But *a* devil. Or demon. Whichever you prefer."

The sizzle of the meat as it was turned released an aroma of burning flesh and fire that, under normal circumstances, would have set everyone's mouth watering.

"Yes, I would imagine the process would have been something like that, only on a much larger yet more focused scale. If it helps, I'm sure she wouldn't have felt much pain."

It didn't help. Torie rolled her eyes, but her mind was spinning.

"Tell us about this brimstone and why you think that indicates it was a demon that did this." She couldn't bring herself to say the word devil again. "I mean, not that we would, but Jasmin and I can summon fire and direct it. That would be hot enough to do this. Why couldn't it be another witch?"

The doctor was shaking his head. "Given time, the fire you could summon might be able to burn at that temperature. But it would most certainly do more ancillary damage than what was contained in the young woman's eyes." He paused, looking at Leo. "Dragon fire could probably do it. I suppose you know where this little fella was at all times, huh?"

Torie was incensed at the thought. "Don't be ridiculous."

Emil held up both hands. "Sorry. I tend to sometimes say things before thinking them through. Still learning what is and is not acceptable behavior in mortal company."

"Back to the brimstone," Jasmin said with a gentle push.

"Oh yes. Among all supernatural creatures, brimstone is unique to those of the demon class. Only demons, and particularly upper class, powerful ones, can wield hellfire, which in turn, leaves brimstone residue."

"That's powerful magic," Jasmin said. "A signature like that can't be easily hidden from us. We just need to know what to look for."

The doctor held up one hand and reached into his pocket with the other. "I am one step ahead of you there." He withdrew two black, glass vials. "I managed to isolate some of the elemental brimstone from the charred bones of the orbital rim. It's in a crystalline form here, so you can add it to an enchanted bauble or token or whatever it is you witches do. You should be able to come up with something capable of tracking the demon; or at least a warning system for whenever it uses its powers again."

"What makes you think it will happen again?" asked Max.

"If you have a demon operating in this town, it's here for a reason," replied the medical examiner.

"Maybe, it stumbled across the human and, well, did what demons do," offered Elric.

"Who said she was human?" replied the doctor.

They all stared at the man, but before anyone could speak, Shawn walked up, dragging Glen behind him.

"Hey guys," he said. "Need any help? We were starting to feel left out over there."

Glen shrugged, giving them an 'I tried' look.

"Nope, the steaks are done so we are all set," Torie said. "Here, why don't you take the vegetables over to the table, someone grab the meat, and Jasmin, why don't you and the good doctor go get the wine and bourbon and bring that out."

She shot her friend a look, but then smiled at the infatuated medical examiner and headed back into the kitchen.

"What kind of doctor is he?" asked Shawn, staring after them.

"He's a medical examiner," Torie replied.

For a moment, she sensed that he was a bit crestfallen. Then he smiled at her, nodding. "You have a really... esoteric group of friends."

She smiled, watching him move to the table carrying two platters of grilled vegetables. While he seemed the same, something was off with him. She made it a point that they would have that conversation first thing in the morning.

"Shawn," she called after him. "Let's have breakfast in the morning. Just the two of us."

He smiled and nodded, placing the food in the center of the outdoor table.

Once everyone was seated, they began passing the food, with wine and laughter following. Torie watched her friends, old and new, as well as her only flesh and blood, and was suddenly overcome with happiness. It was closely followed by a sense of guilt for feeling that way. A young woman had just died, after all, and there was a potential demon loose in her town.

Despite hoping against it, she knew from past experience that another murder was very likely. Why was this happening here in Singing Falls? This town was a peaceful haven for people like her. Why was there always some big bad that decided they wanted to take a bite out of her community?

But deep down, she knew the answer to that. There were so many supernatural beings living in this town, the sheer numbers dictated that certain bad elements would be drawn here as well. Singing Falls sat at the confluence of several ley lines, and while it enhanced magic, it also made them stand out like a spotlight in the dark to any number of creatures looking for an easy meal.

While the town had recently loosened its restrictions on vampires and other, more darker beings, living within its community, she was pretty sure a demon would not be welcomed. Especially going by the way the doctor had described them. That thought triggered something for her. What exactly does a demon look like? She knew what she thought they should look like, but if she had learned anything since moving to this town, it was to throw her preconceived notions about what something was out the window.

"I know that look," Elric whispered, leaning into her. "Your mind is on that body, right?"

She glanced around and then nodded. "I can't help it. What a terrible way to go. We need to find out where this monster is that did this and put a stop to it."

He nodded, chewing slowly on a piece of meat. "Is there a way for you to create multiple talismans from that sample of brimstone? I was thinking, if you can give a bit to all of us, tracking this thing down might go a lot faster."

Torie mulled his words over, knowing that what he said made sense, but also knowing what it could lead to. "I don't know about that. It makes sense, but at the same time, this is an unknown creature; something none of us have ever faced. I can't put you and Max in that kind of situation."

"Oh, but it's okay for you and Jasmin to risk your lives going after a demon."

"We are witches. We have magic to protect us."

"You have no idea what you're up against any more than Max or I. You're flying blind here and just as vulnerable as anyone else."

"We'll discuss this later," she said, noticing they were starting to draw a few curious looks.

Elric didn't respond, just went back to stabbing forkfuls of meat.

"What's going on?" asked Jasmin.

"Oh nothing. Elric was just wondering what I marinated the steak in," Torie replied.

Jasmin was seated between Max and the doctor, and Max immediately leaned over and whispered in her ear. At the same time, Torie saw Fionna lean in and whisper to Glen.

Shifters and their ears.

Luckily, Shawn didn't seem to notice that he was the only one left out of the conversation and was happily working through a gigantic serving of vegetables. He had a fork halfway to his mouth when he stopped, his nose wrinkling.

"What is that smell?" he asked.

He bent down, looking under the table to see Leo working ravenously at a large piece of very well-done meat.

"Did you give the cat that piece of burnt meat? Is that healthy?"

Torie took a peek and saw that somehow Leo had wrangled his own piece of steak. The meat he was eating was still smoking; he had obviously added his own touch of fire to the flesh, burning it almost beyond recognition.

"Well, that's new," Torie said. "Usually, he likes his food…a little more on the rare side."

A beeping sound floated from the kitchen, through the open patio doors.

"That's the monitor system for the house; someone must be at the front door," Torie said.

Both Max and Elric were suddenly on guard.

"That's funny," said Elric. "I didn't…um…*hear* anyone."

"Neither did I," said Max, his nose quivering slightly in the air. "Still don't."

Shawn looked from one to the other at the two men. "Alrighty then. You guys are weird. If no one else is getting the door, I will."

No!" said everyone in unison.

"It's okay, Shawn. There are some very eccentric neighbors in the area and the only time they come out this late at night, unannounced, is if they want to sell us something.

Something we don't want…" said Torie. "You wait here. I know how to get rid of them."

She rose, nodding for Elric to come with her and then gave Jasmin and Fionna a pointed look before glancing Shawn's way. Her friends rose and went to stand next to the boy. Leo hopped onto the table and moved to sit squarely in front of Shawn as well, facing the patio doors.

"Hold up, I'm going with you," said Max, walking inside with Torie and Elric.

"What in the world are people selling around here?" muttered Shawn, rolling his eyes.

Inside, the trio made their way to the door. Before opening it, Torie turned to the men, nodding. They had already half shifted, long claws extended from their fingers as Torie turned the knob, slowly opening the door just a crack.

Outside stood two elderly women, hands clasped together. In their other hands, one held a cane and the other a woven basket resting in the crook of her arm.

They were short, barely reaching five feet tall, with weathered skin and gray hair that each wore straight, the scraggly ends reaching just below their shoulders. They wore dresses that reached mid-calf with wide, black leather belts buckled high on their waists.

"Good evening. May we come in?" said one of them.

Torie glanced at the two men to her right, behind the door.

Max shook his head no then pointed to his nose. Whoever these women were, he couldn't smell them, even at such a close range.

"Well, I'm sorry, but I'm in the middle of a dinner with friends, so it's really not a good time." Torie looked past the women for a car but saw nothing.

"Oh, come now," said the first woman. "Surely, you're not going to listen to two old wolves telling you not to let us in, are you? They are terribly fickle and jittery when it comes to making sound judgement, right, sister?"

"Quite right," said the second woman. "Terrible judges."

Torie stared at them, trying to probe them silently with magic, only to receive nothing in return.

"Oh, that tickled," said the first woman. "If you invite us in, I promise we will explain everything to your liking."

Again, Torie stared before giving a quick glance to Elric and Max.

"I don't think she liked the way you said, 'invite us in'. Maybe she thinks we are vampires," said the second.

"Oh, I assure you we are not. But if you want us to leave, then I guess we have no choice. Of course, if we do, we won't be able to tell you about that awful creature prowling your beautiful little town, burning out young women's eyes."

Chapter Seven

"Everyone, these are our new neighbors that just moved to town. I completely forgot that I invited them to come over tonight if they weren't busy."

Torie gave her friends a look, smiling politely and nodding as they all stood down. All except Fionna that was. Torie could tell she was still on high alert, and she scooted even closer to Shawn, not taking her eyes off the two older women who had walked up to the table.

"My name is Vera," said the first woman. "This is my little sister Corin."

"It's so nice to meet you all," said Corin, her eyes dancing from one figure to the next.

"It's very nice to meet you both," said Jasmin, her tone measured, yet firm.

"Ah, Jasmin. How did we know you'd be here," said Corin.

"My, what a lovely bunch of people. Each of you so… special," said Vera, scanning the group. Her eyes landed on Shawn and then Glen. "Well, mostly."

Torie saw Shawn frown and start to speak. "Shawn, can you do me a huge favor? I just remembered the sisters here have dairy allergies. Would you mind taking my car and just running into town to the grocery store and getting some vegan milk and desserts please? You remember where it is, right?"

He frowned, looking puzzled. "Um, yeah, I guess…"

"Hold on, I'll go with you," offered Glen.

They headed for the kitchen, and Torie mouthed the words *thank you* to Glen as she passed. Once they were out of the kitchen, and she could hear the soft beep of the alarm as the garage door opened, she turned to the sisters.

"Okay, who are you? We aren't going to have long to talk."

Both women were now focused entirely on Leo, who sat on the ground licking his front paw. He did not seem the least bit interested in the women, and that at least made Torie feel a little better; she trusted his instincts implicitly.

Vera, sat down at the table, while Corin occupied herself by slowly walking around the patio, her gaze flitting over the fencing, the pool and the back of the house itself.

"I'm sorry for that little fib," Torie said. "But my son is…not one of us. I don't want him involved in this. But can I offer you anything? Water perhaps?"

"Oh, that would be nice," said Vera. "With ice if you have it."

"Of course. Elric, would you mind?"

The wolf didn't say anything but headed into the kitchen, closing the patio doors after entering.

"How interesting," noted Vera. "The two of you are connected on such a deep level. Why do you even bother with verbal communication? I've never known a wolf to mate with someone outside of their own pack. Let alone a witch."

Torie didn't say anything but stared at the old woman. "How do you know so much about me?"

The woman raised her eyebrows, but it was her sister that answered, still hovering near the back of the house.

"Oh, we know all of you. Tell me, why did you enchant your house? For that matter, why do you have so much space when it is just you and your little cub?"

"I'm not a cub," said Elric as he exited the kitchen, a tray with two glasses of water atop it and a small, silver ice bucket. "Wasn't sure how much ice you wanted. Figured you could help yourself." He sat the tray on the table and moved to stand next to Torie.

"Oh, don't mind my sister," said Vera, reaching for a glass. "To us, all of you are mere children. So young."

"Except for this one," Corin said, moving up behind Dr. Faun. "Aren't you an interesting creature."

"Why don't you tell us something about yourselves." It was Jasmin who spoke up. Her eyes had gone silver as she scanned the sisters with her magic. "Because I am not getting anything from you."

"Same here. No scent. I can't even detect a heartbeat," added Max. His voice was just above a snarl.

"That's because we exist apart from the rest of you supernaturals," said Vera, sipping her water. "We are part of something else."

"We're listening," said Torie.

"We are the Fates," said Vera. "We sisters comprise the watchers on high. It is our responsibility to ensure that nature moves the way that it should; that it is not misinterpreted by human or supernatural."

Torie frowned, shaking her head. "What does that mean? How can someone misinterpret nature?"

"It means bending the course off what is natural and making it something obscene; something unnatural. Like giving vampires the ability to walk in the daylight. Were-wolves the ability to change abasing the cycle of the moon. Ghosts the ability to move back and forth between the veil that separates the living and the dead," said Corin. Her eyes were no longer wandering about the property and were locked with Torie's.

"But…those things happen," said Fionna.

Vera took another small sip and nodded. "Exactly. The laws of nature that govern the supernatural are not the same as those that govern the human world. But they are laws, nonetheless. And lately, they have been slowly eroding in this town of yours."

They stared at the two women, everyone all but holding their breath. To Torie, it sounded as if even the cicadas had ceased to chirp. The even air seemed to grow humid and heavy, what little breeze that reached them from across the high ridge barely cooled now-damp skin.

Jasmin called up her magic, the hum of it vibrating around the patio. In response, Max half shifted again, claws at the ready.

"Why does that sound like a vaguely disguised threat?" she said.

"Easy, witch. We have no quarrel with you. Besides, your power would have little impact on us." said Corin. She waved her hand gently in the air, dismissing Jasmin's magic with a vibration of her own power.

Torie was stunned at the show of power and moved quickly, holding up both hands to stop Max from fully shifting. She knew she had to defuse the tension in the air if she wanted to get any kind of answers out of these women.

"Okay, let's just all take a deep breath and unclench a bit. That includes you, Max. These ladies are here to help us; I think."

"We are. And we are here to help ourselves as well," said Vera.

"And there it is. The Fates are not one to offer anything up freely, unless it directly benefits them." It was Dr. Faun speaking for the first time. He was staring hard at the elderly women, his eyes moving from one to the other and back again.

"Well, we don't all have the option of giving the appearance of being as altruistic as you, Emil," Vera said, offering the sprite a sly smile.

The way these women seemed to know everyone so intimately unnerved Torie, as had the way they had so casually cancelled out Jasmin's magic. She stared at her friend and could see the wheels turning in her head. She silently implored her not to do anything until they had a better understanding of what was going on.

"You're obviously very powerful," said Torie. "What could we possibly offer you in the way of help? You seem to know everything, including information about the demon that killed the young woman in town earlier. That means you already know more than we do."

"You are correct," said Corin. "We observe, but we are severely limited in how we can act. Like us, this demon…as you call it, stands outside of the supernatural hierarchy. We are not able to stop it."

"But *you* can," said Vera. "Maybe."

"Tell us what you know," said Max. His eyes glowed and his voice was little more than a whispered growl.

If his demeanor ruffled the sisters, they didn't show it.

"The demon you seek serves a dark lord. One that once walked these very lands; and has designs on doing so again," said Vera. "But in order to do that, he needs his minion on earth, the demon, to clear the way for him to return."

"And that would be the perversion of nature you were talking about earlier?" asked Torie.

Vera nodded. "The fact that this demon is able to walk among mortals is proof the perversion is happening. But it has a way to go before the monster's dark lord can enter this domain."

"But the things you said that were concerning— vampires walking in daylight, werewolves turning against the cycles of the moon—those have been explained," said Jasmin. "Werewolves are shifters, they aren't constrained to the moon phases. That's just myth. And from what we have come to understand, some vampires that are very, very old can withstand the light of the sun."

Her words made Torie think of Elion; the ages-old vampire who had recently helped them defeat an ancient evil known as a chimera. He had stated there were vampires in the world even older than he who could walk in the daylight.

"Originally, none of that was possible," said Corin. "All supernaturals abided by the law of their species. Then, long ago, that slowly changed. In the beginning, before man, there was only darkness; and within that darkness, lived spirits and things with no name. Once man came along, he gave those things names; in order to warn other men as to what might be lurking in the shadows around them.

"Eventually, the named creatures; vampires, werewolves, banshees, sirens…even witches came to see the humans as a necessity. Something to co-exist with; not wipe out of existence."

"Why would they need humans?" asked Fionna.

"A continually replenishing food source, for one thing," said Dr. Faun.

Torie felt her stomach turn as she stared at him. She didn't like where this was headed.

"That, and the fact that some supernaturals used humans to multiply their numbers," added Vera. "If the human species died off, so too would the vampires, eventually."

"Over time, all this coexistence between humans and supernaturals became the norm in certain places. Communities, much like Singing Falls, began popping up around the world. And most, like Singing Falls, are wonderful communities of acceptance and coexistence," said Corin.

"Most, but not all," added Vera, her tone ominous and dark.

Max growled again. "You're talking about Trinity Cove."

Trinity Cove was the sister town to Singing Falls. It was farther south, at the base of the mountain where Singing Falls was located. It, too, was a community where humans lived alongside the supernatural. But aside from that, it was the polar opposite of Singing Falls. It was a community of perpetual darkness, where creatures prowled the shadows and humans lived in fear. Torie had heard tales of the town, but she had never seen it for herself. Max and Elric had been there, and both were determined never to return.

"That town exists in a nexus, where the world of man and the world of the undead meet. It is hidden from most human eyes, and even the bravest of supernaturals will not go there. If that dark lord has his way, it is what Singing Falls will become," said Vera.

"There are three communities that are ideally located on ley lines that, if their magic were perverted, would allow the dark lord a foothold back into the world of man. His demons will become the dominate forces in this plane, laying waste to all other life forms beneath them," said Corin. "Here, Trinity Cove, and Half Moon Bay."

"Each of these towns have their protectors. But the dark one grows shiftier in how he attacks each," added Vera.

Torie was nodding. "From what I've heard, Trinity Cove is protected by a powerful witch of a very rare blood lineage. Half Moon Bay has Serena to protect its shores. We've met her and have all the faith in the world in her abilities. Who does Singing Falls have?"

The old women's eyes twinkled as they looked from Torie to Jasmin and back again.

"You're kidding, right? I mean, Jasmin yes, but me? I hardly know anything."

"True. You are like the protector of Half Moon Bay. She also came into her power later in life, but she has blossomed. Now it's your time," said Vera.

"Wait, Trinity Cove is under a cover of perpetual darkness," Jasmin said. "Doesn't that mean it's already fallen?"

Corin was shaking her head. "No. The darkness is its protection. It was a master spell cast by the witch who watches over the town. The darkness is a byproduct that was needed to keep the true forces of evil away."

"So that leaves Singing Falls. If this town falls to the perversion of nature, then true evil will have gained a foothold. And once that happens, it may be too late for anyone to stop its spread," said Corin.

"And you can't help us?" questioned Jasmin.

"No. We are very limited in our abilities when it comes to direct conflict. We watch. And when the natural course of things begins to fall to manipulation, we can take on the role of advisor. As needed." Corin's tone let Torie know that there may be more there, but she wasn't sure how to get it out of the older woman.

Turned out, she was lucky enough that there was someone present who did.

"Where is your sister?" said Emil Faun. "The Fates are comprised of three sisters. Where is your third?"

All eyes turned to the sisters as the elder women exchanged looks. Torie felt something unspoken pass between them, and she knew they were weighing what they said next very carefully.

"The demon that is hunting your town is named Nerian. It is seeking something that will aide in the fall of this town," said Corin.

"And what might that be?" I asked.

"Us," said Vera. "And a weapon. If we are killed, then there will be no one to help course-correct nature. It will make it that much easier for evil to walk your streets."

"And you are correct, sprite. There were three of us; but Nerian has succeeded in killing our sister. And now, the demon hunts your streets, looking for our mortal disciples. The young woman who died earlier was one such disciple. By killing them off, Nerian hopes to weaken us and blind us to its movements. Making it that much easier to kill my sister and me."

No one spoke. Everyone stared at the sisters, not daring to breathe.

"There's more, I'm assuming," Torie said. "We, or at least I, have a lot of questions."

Max stepped forward. At some point, he had taken his

phone out of his pocket and was staring at it as he walked forward.

"That might have to wait," he said. "There's a disturbance of some kind in town. Something's happening at the Qwik Stop grocery."

Torie stood up, her heart trip-hammering.

"That's where I sent Shawn."

Chapter Eight

By the time they arrived at the store, Torie had called Shawn no less than seven times, and each time it went to voicemail.

"I should have magicked us there," she said, sitting in the back of Elric's Bronco as he sped towards the store.

"You heard what the sisters said, if that demon thing is near, he will smell your magic. That might put Shawn in even more danger," Jasmin said from the front seat. "Besides, Fionna set off on foot and will get there ahead of us to scout things out."

Max sat in the back scowling. "I don't trust those women."

"That's makes two of us," Elric added, looking briefly at his friend in the rearview mirror.

"It's that wolf instinct," said Jasmin. "And you must admit, something felt off with them. They were definitely holding back about something."

Torie continued to stare at her phone, trying to will it to connect to Shawn. The truth of the matter was, she wasn't sure she cared why the Fates had reached out to them. The fact that there was something in her town hunting people, and they had information on how to stop it, was all she needed. They had faced any number of ghoulish threats together before; this one would be no different.

Only this time it *was* different. Her only child was around, and she couldn't keep images of him being in danger out of her mind. She cared for everyone around her equally, but that was different. All her friends belonged to this supernatural community. They were capable of taking care of themselves.

But what could Shawn do?

He didn't have magic to protect him. He didn't have a hide of thick fur to block the damage from slashing claws or pointed fangs. His nails couldn't pierce the flesh of an attacker, and he would most certainly break a tooth if he tried biting anything harder than a stale crouton. He was helpless in the face of monsters. She had protected him since the day he came into the world, and she knew the day she stopped protecting him would never come.

Especially now that she knew what kinds of creatures truly stalked the shadows.

She was about to try his phone once again when Elric announced they had arrived. He pulled into the parking lot of the shopping mart to be greeted by flashing lights from two of the town's police cars. They were pulled in at a diagonal facing the front entrance.

As they pulled in, Max rushed to the officer in charge of the scene and began questioning him. Torie followed closely but was distracted by a shadowy figure leaning out from a corner of the building and motioning for her and Jasmin.

It was Fionna, and she seemed highly agitated.

Torie and Jasmin hurried to her side, leaving Max and Elric to decipher what the police officers were relaying.

"Fionna, what's going on? Did you see Shawn?" asked Torie worriedly.

Fionna placed both hands on her friend's arms. "First, he seems fine. I was able to sneak in through the vents and got a good look at him. He doesn't seem to be in any danger."

"Well, what is going on?" demanded Jasmin. "Were you able to tell?"

"There's a man in there, acting very weird. He's accosting a young woman. Not sure if this is a domestic situation or something more."

"I have to get in there," said Torie.

"The front entrance is covered by the cops," Fionna replied. "And of course, this would be the one time when neither of them are shifters. Two human cops that look as scared as the cashier worker."

"We can go in through the loading dock," said Jasmin. "We just need to make sure the cops don't burst in and shoot us accidentally."

"I can try and let Max know what's going on," said Fionna. "You guys get in there and see what you can do."

With that, she shifted to her squirrel form and sprinted around the building. While Torie could read the minds of shifters in their animal form, she knew that they could not communicate telepathically with species outside of their own; so hopefully her presence alone would be enough to let Max know something was afoot with Torie and Jasmin.

Thinking about that gave her an idea and she reached out to Elric. Even though he was in human form, they still shared a special rapport; one that she could tap into and speak with. She closed her eyes briefly, pushing her thoughts out.

"Elric knows what we are up to. He's going to figure out a way to have Max get his officers to stand down momentarily," said Torie.

Jasmin squinted. "Is that all he said?"

Torie shrugged. "He said we should stay put until we can figure out what we're up against."

Jasmin gave her a look that Torie brushed off. "That's my son in there, Jasmin."

"I know," her friend replied. "What are we waiting for?"

They made their way over to the loading dock and ascended the concrete stairs. Even though it was late, the back entrance remained open, and they eased through the creaky metal door into an open storage room. From there, they headed for the door that led to a large walk-in refrigerator on one side, and entrance into the store on the other.

"Wait," said Jasmin. She closed her eyes and held up both hands, whispering a concealment spell that cloaked both of them.

Together, they crept into the store making their way through the limited aisles until they could see the checkout area.

"We're inside. I can see the checkout girl, she looks terrified. There's a man dressed in a green jogging suit. He's holding a knife and saying something to her." Torie broadcast her thoughts to Elric and Fionna, knowing they would relay what was being said to Max.

"Can you make out what he's saying?" Torie whispered. She knew Jasmin's spell would protect them from being seen, but it would only do so much to muffle sound.

"No. We need to get closer. Of course, all the noise coming from outside isn't helping."

The sound of the sirens coupled with the commotion of the officers barking orders seemed to fill the store. Torie was looking about frantically, and then she saw him.

Shawn.

He was standing at the entrance to an aisle just behind the man with the knife. He was turned sideways and slowly making his way towards the man. In one hand he held a can of something that Torie could not make out. But she knew what he meant to do as he stealthily took another step forward.

No. She began to panic inside. There was one of those oval mirrors mounted above the register where the ceiling and the wall met, and Torie knew the knifeman would see her son well before he was close enough to launch a canned goods attack.

She held out her hand, motioning in Shawn's direction, and then clasped her fingers into a fist. In response, a few of the items on the shelf next to him fell to the floor with a clatter. The knife wielder turned quickly, brandishing it in Shawn's direction and yelling menacingly at the young man.

Torie held her breath as Shawn complied with the man's demands, dropping his makeshift weapon and getting down on his knees. Torie could see his hands shaking and it made her heart break. Her eyes hardened as she focused on the man threatening him.

She was going to enjoy making him pay for this.

Jasmin's hand on her wrist stopped her from casting a spell in his direction. When she turned to question Jasmin, her friend was pointing to her eyes, and then to the man with the knife. Torie stared at the man, and then saw what Jasmin had seen.

The man's eyes were black. Not the iris, but the entire orb; it was black as a starless night.

That changed things, but it also added a sense of urgency that Torie had not felt before. She felt her back break out in a cold sweat as she contemplated just what the man could be. Was he a supernatural or was he being possessed by one?

"Demon?" she whispered to Jasmin.

"I don't know. We don't know enough about them. Maybe this guy is being used?"

"Or maybe he is the actual demon. We don't know what they look like."

Elric's words flashed through her mind, and all she could do was hope that in her haste she hadn't put her son in even more danger.

"We need to get closer. I need to hear what he is saying," said Torie.

Together, they made their way towards the front of the store, protected by Jasmin's cloak. Once within earshot, they stopped moving, trying to discern what the man was saying to the young cashier.

"…You're lying! Tell me or I promise I'll make you scream with pain you have never experienced!" His voice was loud and tremulous. His hand was shaking as well, the point of the knife quivering in his grasp.

"I promise you, I don't know what you're talking about. I just work here…I don't know who you're talking about. Please…I just want to go home." The young woman was tearing up, fear oozing from every pore in her body.

She glanced around frantically, her eyes cutting to the flashing lights outside the store window.

"They aren't coming in here. At least not in time to help you," he said, following her eyes with his black ones.

But then, the cashier did something that surprised the

two witches. She looked at them. Her eyes grew wide, and her mouth dropped as she stared.

"What are you looking at?" said the man, the paranoia in his tone rising as he turned in their direction. His black eyes dropped to a squint. He turned back to see the cashier still staring toward them, and slowly took a few tentative steps in their direction. His head was cocked to one side, and Torie could see his nostrils flare.

Was he...smelling for them?

Then, his eyes focused on their direction. He snarled, dropping his knife.

"I might not be able to see you...but I can smell you," he growled.

His voice literally became a growl as he raised both arms and began to shift into the form of a very large grizzly bear. He dropped to all fours and unleashed a roar that rattled the walls. Head lowered, he charged at the witches, one gigantic paw clearing the displays in front of him.

Torie and Jasmin waited, preparing to drop the cloak and hit the beast with their own magic, when the cashier vaulted over the counter, landing beside the bear and drawing a six-inch knife from a leather holster strapped to her leg. In the blink of an eye, the steel flashed from under her white store apron, and she slashed at the side of the bear.

The beast roared in response, turning on her and rearing onto its hind legs, all fur, fang and claw as it towered over the woman. She had her knife in front of her and any trace of fear from earlier had completely vanished.

Before Torie or Jasmin could act, the front doors flew open and two large wolves rushed in, launching themselves at the bear shifter. The grizzly roared in surprise and then pain as Max sank his teeth into its hindside while Elric leapt onto the creature's back, biting deep into the base of its neck.

The shifter howled in pain, throwing the wolves off as it ran towards the front, crashing through the large floor-to-ceiling windows on the side of the store and speeding off across the parking lot, Max and Elric hot on its heels. The two police officers standing next to their patrol cars were too dumbfounded to speak as they watched, mouths agape, at three very large animals roaring off into the night.

Torie and Jasmin looked at one another, then turned their attention to the girl and Shawn. Shawn had raced to the young cashier's side and was waving one hand in front of her face. Still cloaked in magic, they approached the two and saw that the young woman appeared to be in some kind of catatonic state. She stood perfectly still, staring straight ahead through eyes that were pale and sightless.

Shawn was starting to panic as he ran his hands through his hair, looking around for help.

Jasmin nodded her head at the front of the store, motioning for Torie to follow her. They stepped outside, where Jasmin then dropped the cloaking spell. Once visible, they rushed back into the store, with Torie calling out for Shawn.

He turned to face them, rushing to hug his mother.

"Mom! What are you doing here?"

"Max got the call that there was a disturbance here from his officers. When I realized it was where I sent you, we rushed right over. Honey, what happened?"

His confusion almost left him speechless as he shook his head. "I honestly don't know where to begin. But we need to help this woman; she's in deep shock or something." And then...he looked around at the carnage in the store, and at the shattered window. "And I can't explain it because I'm not sure I believe what I saw. I mean, I couldn't have seen what I saw. There was a bear. Only, it wasn't a bear; it was a man that was threatening us…and then it was a bear."

Torie and Jasmin exchanged looks as he continued to stare at everything around him, perplexed.

"Honey, are you hurt? Do we need to get you checked out? Maybe you hit your head?"

"No, Mom, I didn't hit my head. I just…I'm not sure what happened is all."

"I think I can hear the siren of an ambulance headed this way," Torie said. "Why don't you step outside, get some air? Jasmin and I are going to bring this lady out as well."

Shawn was still muttering to himself, but slowly began to plod towards the doors as his mother and Jasmin turned to face the girl. She was still staring straight ahead, eyes pale and locked onto nothing.

Torie snapped her finger in front of her face, to no avail. "What is going on here?" she asked.

Jasmin shook her head. "Not sure, but we need to snap her out of this before the paramedics get here. Did you see the way she moved? How she attacked that shifter?"

"Yeah. It was like she became a completely different person."

"Let me try something," Jasmin said, raising her hand in front of the girl. She closed her eyes and called on her magic.

"Let she who is lost, now be found,
and find your own freewill no longer be bound."

Immediately, her eyes cleared, and she looked around frantically. "What? What just happened? Who are you?"

Torie placed her hands on the woman's shoulders,

trying to calm her. Then, with a sudden stiffening of her spine, the girl's eyes paled again.

"Bring her to us," she said calmly.

Both Torie and Jasmin were startled. The voice that came from the young woman's mouth was not her own. It was Vera, speaking through her.

"If you don't bring her to us, you will have another dead body on your hands before morning," Vera continued.

Then, as quickly as it happened, her eyes cleared again, and the witches found themselves staring into the panicked gaze of a woman who burst into tears, clinging desperately to them.

Chapter Nine

"I'm going to scout around; make sure there aren't any other shifters we need to worry about in the area. I'll meet you back at your house in a bit," said Fionna. With that, she shifted into her squirrel form and disappeared around the back of the store, heading for the wooded area beyond.

It had taken some convincing to get the girl into the car with them. Finally, when Jasmin told her the man who had threatened her was still on the loose, she agreed to go back to Torie's house. She didn't remember the man shifting into a bear, just that he was standing there threatening her with a knife. After that, she remembered Torie and Jasmin shaking her; but nothing in between.

Her name was Erin Breck and she had moved to Singing Falls just a few weeks ago to house sit for her cousin for the summer. Her cousin was backpacking through Europe and needed someone she trusted to watch after the house and keep it running. Erin stated that as soon as she stepped foot off the bus, she felt an odd sense of peace here in Singing Falls.

That was until she was threatened at knifepoint while working her cousin's job at the Qwik Stop. She had told them, in a monotone voice, that that was how her cousin was able to get the entire summer off without losing her job; finding a replacement that was as trustworthy as she was and worked just as hard.

She sat silently in the back of the car, wedged next to an equally stunned Shawn. Torie worried that what he had seen might have been more than his mind could process; but the few things he had said led her to think that maybe he was rationalizing himself into not believing that a man had turned into a bear right before his eyes.

The fact that Erin didn't remember seeing anything like that worked in Torie's favor as well.

"You know, these are the mountains. There are all kinds of wild animals running around the area. Bears, mountain lions, wolves. You name it. Sometimes they can wander into town," she had told Shawn once he was in the car.

Jasmin had taken the time to cloud the police officers' minds, making them understand that they couldn't possibly have seen their sheriff and his friend turn into large wolves and rush into the store.

Because that would be just plain crazy.

Torie didn't like the idea of altering anyone's memories, but she knew what had happened was not the kind of conversation anyone not a member of the supernatural community was ready to have.

At some point, she knew they all needed to have a conversation with Max about hiring only shifters to work under him. That, of course, came with its own set of issues she didn't like.

Wouldn't doing that be a form of discrimination? But did those ethics outweigh the potential safety of those involved? The officers who had responded could have easily been killed had they charged into the store unknowingly.

Torie eyed the two youths in the rearview mirror as she drove. They were each peering out their windows, lips occasionally moving along with an internal monologue as they continued to try and convince themselves of what was and was not real.

They weren't focusing on the adults in the front seat at all, and Jasmin took the opportunity to slowly wiggle the fingers of one hand, drawing up a magical, sound-blocking partition between the front of the car and the back.

"Don't look over at me, just keep focused on driving," she said casually as she glanced out the passenger window.

Torie understood what she had done and adjusted her hands on the steering wheel, carefully speaking without giving the indication she was.

"Jasmin, I don't know what was scarier back there. The fact that a bear shifter did that in public, or that this cashier was taken over by a Fate and then used as a human weapon against said bear shifter."

Jasmin trailed a finger along the glass absentmindedly. "I am pretty sure your two houseguests just went body surfing in that young woman. But somehow, they did it without using magic. At least not any form of magic I'm familiar with."

"They might have saved her…or us, from that shifter."

"By completely taking over someone's body? Suppressing their will like that? There is a lot more to these women than they are sharing."

"I agree. But what can we do about it?"

"Well, for starters, did you have to open your home to them? Let them stay the night? How are you going to explain that to Shawn?"

Torie hesitated, checking the mirror to see that Shawn and Erin were still in their own little worlds. "I think after tonight, I need to tell him everything. I can't have my son questioning his own sanity."

Jasmin didn't say anything, just turned away from the window to stare at her friend. "And if he doesn't accept that?"

Torie shrugged. "He has no choice. I'm not using some spell to alter his memories or something like that."

"Why do you think the sisters want us bringing Erin to them?" Jasmin said, clearly trying to pivot the conversation. "We just said we don't know anything about them. What if they try to hurt her?"

"Then we stop them. They said it themselves; they can't do much against our magic. Something tells me they need us more than we need them."

Jasmin was nodding. "Definitely. The only way to find out what exactly is going on with them is to play along. For now."

After a beat of silence, another thought occurred to Torie. "Did you see how she looked at us back there in the store?" She tilted her head towards the girl in the backseat. "Somehow, she saw us through your cloaking spell. Does that happen a lot?"

"It can...with certain humans that possess a bit of psychic power. Usually, they don't know they even have it until something opens them up to the world around them. That could be what we are dealing with here."

Torie wasn't convinced but didn't say anything more. They made the rest of the drive to her house in silence. She kept glancing at her phone that was clipped into the heads-up display on the dash. No message from Elric yet. For all she knew, they could still be chasing that bear across the mountains.

That was what she chose to believe at least. Elric had fought and survived far worse than a grizzly shifter.

They pulled into the long, circular drive outside the house and climbed out of the car. Erin appeared a bit dazed, staring at the large home.

"You...live here?" she asked.

Torie nodded. "Don't worry. It's far comfier than it looks."

Erin started forward, then hesitated, running her hand along her store-branded frock. "I just realized I don't have anything to wear. I should go back to my cousins and at least get a change of clothing."

"Don't worry about that," said Torie. "I have plenty of sweatpants and pajama sets you can choose from. There's a guest bath filled with them. You're welcome to whatever you need."

"Our friend is the sheriff investigating what happened tonight," added Jasmin. "As soon as he says everything is clear, we can take you back to your cousin's. How's that sound?"

"Can I shower as well?" she asked.

"You don't even have to ask that," said Torie. "Jasmin, why don't you show her to one of the guest suites upstairs. Maybe the one on the opposite side of the house from our other guests? Then join us on the patio to finish our little conversation."

Jasmin nodded and led Erin into the house, through the entry, and up one side of the grand, double-sided staircase.

"Shawn, I think there are some things we need to discuss," Torie said. "Probably the sooner the better."

He looked at her, his face still a puzzled mask. "Yeah, I've been saying that."

A pang of guilt passed through Torie, and she could feel the heat of rising redness as it flushed her cheeks. "Why don't we go into the kitchen. I'm sure you could use a cup of hot tea to help calm your nerves after tonight."

He followed her in, letting out a deep sigh. "I don't suppose you have anything stronger?"

She laughed, shaking her head. "Not for a couple more years for you."

His laughter in response filled her heart with pangs of longing and fear as she turned and wrapped him in her arms.

"Mom, I'm okay," he said softly.

"I know. I just hate that you had to experience that." She sniffed and pulled herself away from him as she reached for the kettle to fill it with water. "Can you get the cups for me?"

"Sure," he said, opening an upper cabinet.

As he reached in, one of the cups shifted and fell forward, past his arm and towards the floor. With a gasp he reached for the cup, but to no avail. Before it hit the floor, it stopped in midair, floating just outside of his reach.

Torie watched in awe as he raised his empty hand and directed the cup safely to the countertop.

"Shawn…" she said.

He took a deep breath. "Yeah. That's what I needed to talk to you about. Things like this have been happening lately; and I don't know why."

Her mouth hung open as she stared first at her son, then the cup, and back to her son.

"I didn't know who to talk to about it," he said, plopping down on one of the barstools at the edge of the island.

"I thought, at first, I was losing my mind. But it kept happening. All I could think was I needed to get away from school, go somewhere…safe. You were the first person I thought of; I'm sorry if I'm scaring you."

The tremble in his voice, the wetness welling in his eyes as he looked away from her, hurt her more than she could have ever imagined.

"But now, after what I thought I saw in the store tonight…I'm back to thinking maybe I am losing my mind. But…you saw that just now, right? I wasn't imagining it?"

She moved to stand next to him just as Jasmin walked into the room.

"Okay, Erin seems to be settling in and is in the shower now. I checked in on our guests and they weren't in their rooms. Maybe——" She stopped speaking as the tension in the room washed over her. "What's going on in here?"

Torie placed a hand on her son's shoulder and tried to muster a smile. Then, she held out her hand and called to the cup. In a flash, it disappeared from the island, only to reappear in her hand.

"It looks like Shawn has inherited a bit of magic," she said.

His eyes grew wide as he stared at his mother. "How… how did you do that?"

"I'm a witch," she replied. "And, while I don't know how it would be possible, I think maybe you are as well."

Chapter Ten

Jasmin stared at Torie, narrowing her eyes. "You know that isn't possible."

"How do we know it's not? If you had asked me when I first arrived in town, I would have said that it's not possible for a man to turn into a wolf. Or a bear," Torie answered. "I would have said that it wasn't possible for witches to exist."

"Mom, I still don't understand. Do you know what's happening to me? And you're...a witch?" Shawn asked. "And how did you just do that?" He was pointing at the cup as she sat it back on the island.

Torie cast a glance at her friend before answering.

"Shawn, it appears that I inherited more than just my eye color from my mother. She was a witch. A hex witch to be exact. It's something that is passed down in our family from mother to daughter on their fortieth birthday. Now it looks like I've passed it on to you."

"Torie, he's not forty," said Jasmin, "And he isn't female. This isn't possible."

Torie looked at her and held the cup up. "Then how do you explain this?" She dropped it and watched as Shawn jumped, reaching for it. When it crashed to the floor, splintering into pieces, she and Shawn stared at it, then looked at one another. "What happened? Why didn't you catch it?"

"I don't know," he said. "I told you I can't control it; it just kind of happens out of the blue."

"Jasmin, I know what I saw. If it wasn't magic, then what?" Torie questioned.

"Wait, can we go back to a man turning into a bear? Are you now saying that happened?" said Shawn.

Before she could answer, a broom and dustpan flew into the room, zipping past Torie as they set about cleaning up the broken mug. After dumping the pieces into a garbage pan, they returned to the utility closet.

Shawn was pointing at the closet door, then at his mother.

"That," she said, "was an example of magic. Like I said, I am a witch. As an experiment, Jasmin and I enchanted the kitchen to be self-cleaning."

"So…you're a witch too?" he said, pointing at Jasmin.

"I am," she said, tentatively.

He sat in silence, staring straight ahead. A couple of times he opened his mouth to speak, but nothing came out.

"Honey, there's a lot to talk about, but we don't have to get into it all now," Torie said.

"What about Fionna? Is she a witch as well?" He was still staring at the counter as he spoke.

Torie exchanged a quick look with Jasmin before she answered. "No. She is a squirrel shifter."

This made him look up at her, his eyebrows arched. There was another question in his eyes, and Torie didn't need him to verbalize it in order to know what it was.

"Elric is…a werewolf. And so is Max."

"Was that them at the store? The ones that fought the bear?"

This realization made him stand; his spine stiff as he ran both hands through his hair. He steadied himself, and Torie could see he was trying to control his breathing.

"So, everyone in your life is…something other than they appear?" he said.

"Well, Glen is human," said Jasmin.

He began pacing back and forth, his lips moving as he mumbled to himself. Then he stopped, his head snapping around to Torie.

"Did Dad know? Oh my God, is he…?" he stammered.

"Yes," she said, before quickly shaking her head. "And no. Yes, he found out, and no, he's not a supernatural. He's one hundred percent human." She wasn't about to go into the whole affair with a fae bit. That was not something she wanted to recount, and definitely not something Shawn needed to hear.

"Were you ever planning to tell me any of this?" he asked. "I mean, if I weren't in the position I was in earlier, would you have told me?"

Torie hesitated. In her mind, she had had this conversation with her son a million times. But now that it was happening, it felt almost too real. Too harmful to the dynamics they had always shared. But she also had to remind herself that he wasn't a child anymore.

"Yes. I would have, eventually. You will always be in my life; so that means you deserve to know everything. I just didn't think it would be like this. I thought I'd have time to craft the perfect moment."

"You know, maybe I should just go back to——" Jasmin started, thumbing towards the door as she headed back out.

"No, stay," Shawn replied. "I mean, I have a lot to think about. Way too many questions to even verbalize right now. I think I need that tea."

"Of course, baby. Coming right up," said Torie, moving to finish what she had started.

"So, you and Gran are both witches. And you pal around with witches and…werewolves." He shook his head. "Werewolves. What else is real?"

Jasmin swallowed. "Well, just about everything you've ever been told wasn't real…probably is. Vampires, ghosts, fae, trolls; you name it, and we've most likely encountered it."

"And are they everywhere, or just in this town?"

"Well, they can exist anywhere in the world, but there are certain areas that seem to attract them. Singing Falls is one of those areas."

"Like the Hellmouth from *Buffy*," he said, his voice trailing off.

"No that would be Trinity Cove," said Jasmin, before Torie could give her a steely look. "What? It is…"

Shawn's brow furrowed and he was about to ask something else when they were interrupted by someone clearing their throat, causing Jasmin to jump.

Turning, they saw the two elderly sisters standing in the entrance to the kitchen, side by side.

"I swear if they keep that up, I'm putting a bell around their necks," mumbled Jasmin.

"Are they…you know?" said Shawn to his mother.

"Something like that, yes," she replied. "Hello, Vera. Corin. We were wondering where you were."

"Did you bring her?" Corin asked, her eyes all but sparkling in the low light.

"She's in the shower. She'll be down shortly," said Jasmin. "In the meantime, would you like some tea?"

"No thank you. But water would be good," said Vera.

"Hey, can you fly? Like on a broom or something?" Shawn asked, wheeling on his mother.

"What? No, of course not," she replied.

"Well, not yet," said Corin, staring at them.

No one spoke as Torie and Jasmin turned to stare at the two sisters. Vera gave Corin a look that the witches were all too familiar with; one they had shared with each other many times when one had said something they shouldn't have.

"Forgive my sister," said Vera, squinting hard at the other Fate. "She gets confused as to what she is saying sometimes."

Corin's body stiffened; her sister may as well have jabbed her in the ribs with her elbow.

"Oh, you're so right, sister. What was I thinking. Forgive me. You see, without our third sister, our vision is not complete. It's hard to tell sometimes what is, from what will be, from what was," Corin replied with a smile."

"Okay, I'm not quite sure what that means, but I'm betting we can get into that later," said Jasmin. "For now, why don't you fill us in on what you want with that girl. And tell us why you thought it was okay to possess her the way you did."

"Possess her? What are you talking about?" said Vera.

Just then, as if on cue, Erin walked into the room. She was wearing a pair of red and gray pajamas and fluffy, green slippers. She started to speak, but then her eyes locked on the two elderly sisters. Her brow furrowed under a look of surprise, and then crept up in wonder. Once again, her eyes turned to a light gray before flashing back to their normal, dark hue.

She rushed forward, throwing her arms around the two women, burying her head against them. The two women patted her back and whispered to her as her body shook with tears.

"I thought I was going to die," she managed to get out, wiping at her eyes as she broke their embrace.

"But you didn't, and that's what matters," said Corin.

Jasmin shot a questioning look to Torie. "Well, that wasn't what I was expecting."

"I was locked. I couldn't switch over," said Erin. "Something kept me locked and I couldn't respond. Not until I saw these women——" she nodded toward Torie and Jasmin, "——and the bear shifted and moved to attack them. Then I was able to act on my own."

Shawn snapped around. "Wait, you were in the store? Were you the reason all those cans suddenly fell off the shelf? I was trying to help…"

Torie turned to her son. "Yes, that was us. But you must realize I was afraid you were going to do something and get yourself hurt. Or worse."

"We can talk about that later," said Jasmin. "Right now, we need to find out what is going on." She turned to face the shifters. "Was that bear shifter the demon?"

"Absolutely not," answered Corin. "Talk about possession, that shifter was an agent working for Nerian. That demon has a way of enslaving supernatural beings with weaker minds."

"So then, who is this girl to you?" asked Jasmin. Then she turned to Erin. "And I'm sorry, I don't mean to talk about you like you aren't standing right here. But, just a while ago, you didn't know anything that was going on with you and had no memory of that shifter."

"It's okay," said Erin. Her demeanor had changed considerably after seeing the two Fates. Granted, she was still wrecked with emotions, but she carried her body completely differently. "I can see where the confusion comes into play."

"I think we need to sit down for this conversation," said Vera.

They followed Torie out of the kitchen to the large, great room and took up seating around one of the many fireplaces that graced the home. Shawn started to turn for the stairs that led to the upper floor guest suites, but Torie stopped him, and motioned for him to follow.

The patio door chimed as Fionna walked in, nodding to everyone. "I didn't find any trace of more shifters around the store. I think that bear shif——" She stopped, eying Shawn.

"No more secrets," Torie said, motioning for everyone to find a place to sit. "He knows. Oh, I forgot the water..."

But just as she began to push herself out of her favorite club chair, she heard the refrigerator opening as well as a cupboard. Two trays floated into the room; one carried four bottles of water, and the second contained a couple of wine glasses and an open bottle of red.

"Okay, what the heck?" said Jasmin. "We aren't in the kitchen...how is this happening?"

The two Fates exchanged looks but neither of them said anything. Shawn stared wide-eyed as the tray with the water floated before him. He reached out a hand and gingerly retrieved the water.

"Thank you...? I guess," he said, staring at the tray as it floated around serving the sisters and Erin.

Torie and Jasmin took the wine, and each poured a heavy glass before taking a soothing sip.

"One weird, magical thing at a time," Torie said. "First, we need to hear what the sisters have to say. What does all of this have to do with Nerian and that dead girl we found earlier?"

Shawn's eyes widened at the mention of a dead girl, but Torie gave him a quick shake of her head.

"That girl was my sister," said Erin. "Well, not by blood, but in calling. We are both disciples of the Fates." Her eyes grew misty, and she cast them downward. "Or at least we were."

Vera leaned forward, clasping the young woman's hand. "Your sister died bravely. She didn't tell him anything."

"How can you be certain?" asked Erin.

"Because if Nerian knew where we were, we would all be dead by now," stated Corin.

"So, you've told us what you are, and that Nerian is after you, but how do these girls come into the picture? Why are they in danger?" asked Jasmin.

"The disciples are more than just our eyes on the ground, so to speak," said Vera. "They are the chosen few with the potential to ascend."

"Ascend? Into what?" asked Jasmin.

Erin looked at the two sisters and smiled; clasping the hands of the women sitting next to her.

"Into the next Fate," she said, her voice filled with hope.

Torie opened her mouth to respond but was drowned out by the sudden crashing of the front door as it flew open. She leapt to her feet, stepping between the entrance to the great room and her son as magic collected in a blue swirl around her fists.

She dropped her power as soon as she recognized Max bursting into the room. In his arms he held a very bloody Elric.

"Somebody! Help him!" he cried.

Chapter Eleven

The shock of what they were seeing wore off and the room erupted into chaos. Moving incredibly quickly for their age, the sisters vacated the couch, and Erin quickly threw the pillows arranged on it onto the floor. Max carefully laid his friend on the couch as Jasmin and Torie rushed to his side.

"What happened?" demanded Torie, taking stock of the bloodied form of the man she loved.

"We chased that bear shifter into the high country and were ambushed...by something. Something I didn't get a good look at. I smelled something...like burning rubber, and then this creature dropped out of nowhere it seemed. It was fast and strong and before I knew what happened, Elric was all but split open by it." He was panting hard, running his hands through his hair as he looked at the mangled body on the couch. "There was a flash of orange, and Elric shifted back into his human form. I didn't think, I just scooped him up and ran as fast as I could."

Elric coughed, blood erupting from his mouth. He

moaned low in the back of his throat, and then screamed in pain.

Torie reached out to grasp her lover, placing a reassuring hand on his chest, only to withdraw it quickly. "He's burning up."

"I'm calling Glen!" Jasmin said.

"He will be dead before she gets here," said Corin, staring at the man. "He's been burned by Nerian. I'm surprised he's still breathing."

"We have to do something," said Jasmin. She held out both hands and began to hum softly. A glow enveloped her arms in soft, amber light, before spreading to the werewolf bleeding out on Torie's couch. She bit her cheek in a grimace, tilting her head to one side. "So…hot. He's trying to heal, but as soon as he does, the heat inside him just burns his organs again. I don't know how long he can last."

Vera turned to Torie; her eyes filled with compassion. "It isn't his time. But my sister and I cannot interfere."

Torie spun to look at Elric's writhing figure. She was filled with love and fear. This was the first man she had met who accepted her fully for who she was; didn't try to change her, or worse…make her feel like she needed to change herself. And the thought of losing him was more than she could bear.

She felt a surge of adrenaline, and with it, magic. It flowed through and out of her, consuming her like a black hole. She gave in, letting her power sweep her off the floor until she hovered in the air, a blue nimbus surrounding her. Her eyes blazed with ethereal energy as she held a hand over her beloved.

"I call on the spirits, from where only the light looms,
to cleanse the fire from this wolf's wounds."

And with those words spoken, she shoved her hand into Elric's chest, passing through skin and bone to grab at the unnatural fire that burned within him.

Elric screamed as she grabbed at the mark the demon had seared into him. Torie screamed at pain she had never known before.

She pulled her hand out, and in her fist, she held a black smoke that pulsed with black magic. It tried to expand, threatening to blow her hand apart in the process, but she gritted her teeth and held fast to the dark magic. Holding out her other hand, she spoke through gritted teeth.

"Vials from Dr. Faun!"

The two vials the medical examiner had given her and Jasmin instantly appeared in her hand. Focusing her will, she slammed her hands together, forcing the black fire she had extracted from Elric into the vials. Then, with a flash of light and magic, she sealed them shut, containing the darkness within.

Then, as the effort of what she had just done caught up with her, Torie's head sagged as her magic left her body, letting her drop. Shawn was at her side almost instantly, catching her and lowering her gently to the floor.

"Help!" he screamed, succumbing to the sudden panic that washed over him.

"She's going to be fine, child," said Corin, placing her hand gently on his shoulder. "What your mother just did was…nothing short of miraculous." She gave her sister a quick glance before returning her gaze to the distraught young man.

He cradled Torie's head, his eyes overflowing with tears. She moaned, slowly opening her eyes to look up into his.

"Hey, you…what's happening? Why are you crying?"

She sat up, quickly, reaching for his face. "Did someone hurt you?"

He smiled, nuzzling into her palm. "No, silly. I was afraid you were…hurt."

She smiled up at him before her eyes grew wide. "Elric! Is he…"

"He's alive," called Jasmin from beside the couch.

"He will be fine; thanks to you," added Vera.

Shawn helped Torie to her feet so she could get a better look at her boyfriend. He had shifted to his wolf form and was curled up tightly on the couch. Jasmin was placing a blanket over him as Torie moved closer.

"He shifted into his wolf form as soon as you pulled that fire out of him," said Jasmin. "He will undoubtedly heal faster this way."

Shawn was staring at his mother with his arms outstretched at his side, his face a mask of amazement. "Mom, I can't believe what I just saw. That was like, super-hero-level stuff you just did!"

"All in a day's work," she replied. "You stick around Singing Falls long enough, there's no telling what you might see."

"Well, if the young man won't take you up on that, perhaps we might," said Corin, giving a slight wink to her sister.

Torie ignored the remark, turning to Max instead. "Can you tell us anything at all about this, Nerian, that attacked you? Where did it happen?"

Max shook his head. "It all happened so fast. One minute we were closing in on that bear shifter, the next, this thing just dropped down on us. We were near…" His voice trailed off and he stared at the group.

"What is it?" asked Jasmin. "Where were you?"

The wolf began to pace, concentration burning on his features. Then he stopped, looking up to address everyone.

"We were chasing the bear, and were so intent on it, that we never bothered to check our surroundings, where we were. That bear led us to the edge of the Black Pit."

Fionna took in a sharp breath, her eyes widening as she released it in a hiss. The two sisters exchanged knowing looks, their eyes darkening.

"Okay, I'll bite, what is this Black Pit thing?" asked Shawn.

"It is an area deep in the mountains that shifters and most other supernatural creatures will not tread," said Max. "It is a cursed place."

"What do you mean by cursed?" asked Torie. "As in magic?"

Fionna was shaking her head. She crossed her arms, hugging herself before she spoke. "No, it is not magic; something else. The official name of the site is the Devil's Tramping Ground. It is surrounded by dense, almost impassable thick forestry. But once you get through, there is a small clearing, and inside that clearing is a path that forms a circle about fifty feet across. It is completely barren; nothing grows on the ground inside that circular path or on its periphery. Locals that were brave enough to approach have tried for years to seed the path and get the woods to grow over it, but to no avail. Nothing can live in that ground."

Torie glanced at Jasmin. "Did you know about this place?"

She shrugged. "Local legend among humans. They claim the path was created because it is where the Devil himself comes to walk the Earth in circles while ruminating on his dark plans for mankind. Again, local legend."

"Well, all I know is that I definitely remember feeling disoriented once we got closer to it, and the sense of revulsion was almost overpowering. That was how this demon of yours got the jump on us, now that I think about it," said Max.

"Did you actually see this devil path?" Torie asked.

He shook his head. "No. But something definitely felt...off."

"I've seen it. Once as a child my cousin and I went there on a dare." Fionna's voice was meek and low, barely a tremble. It was a tone none of the other women had ever heard her use. "I've heard other supernaturals describe getting the same feeling around it as Max. It's a black circle of dirt. Perfectly round and dark. But it wasn't the appearance that was so freaky; it was the way I felt. Even in the woods leading up to the Pit. My stomach was tied in knots. We smaller, prey shifters, live and die by our instincts. And every instinct I had was telling me to run from that place and never look back. Everything about the Pit screamed death and pain. I don't know what created such a place, but it was beyond unnatural. It felt like it was carved from pure blackness. And the worst part was the constant feeling of being watched by something."

She hugged herself at the memory, and Torie could see the effect remembered fear was having on her body.

"Do you remember how to get to this place? This Pit or the Devil's Tramping Ground. Whatever you want to call it?" Torie asked.

Before Fionna could answer, Vera spoke up. "Torie, there are some places in this world where we are not meant to tread. The place they are describing is one of those. Even for witches of your abilities, it is not safe."

Everyone, including her sister, turned to face her.

"That is not for us to advise," said Corin.

"Do you know what this place is?" asked Jasmin.

Corin sighed. "What it is? No. All we know is that it was created during a time before there was a separation between the world of the supernatural and that of man. It was created, for whatever purpose, by the Old Ones. The Originals. The Unnamed. And it acts as a tether between this world and the realm the demon hunting us is from."

"Interesting," said Jasmin. She turned to Torie, a large grin on her face. "Road trip?"

Torie was nodding. "Most definitely."

"Hold up," said Shawn. "Didn't you hear what Fionna and these women just said? It's not a place to tread. You're just going to disregard all of that?"

"Shawn, son…you know how when you were a child and your father and I would tell you not to do something for your own good? But you would do it anyway? Well, it's payback time."

The look on his face was almost comical, if there hadn't been an underlying shadow of fear and pain.

Torie reached for her son. "Hey, it's okay. I was just trying to lighten the mood. Jasmin and I have faced worse than some so-called demon. We'll be careful."

"This is definitely not their first time at the rodeo," said Fionna. "But still, that place just feels…rotten. I get physically ill the closer I get to it, and I'm betting it will be the same for Max. You'd be going in alone."

Torie considered her friend's words. "Maybe. Maybe not." She turned to Jasmin and gave her a wink. "After all, sprites aren't shifters."

Jasmin looked at her, squinting her eyes. "No. Not happening."

"Oh, come on. I saw the way you looked at him during

dinner. And more importantly, the way he looks at you. Besides, Fionna makes a good point about us going in alone. We may need back up," Torie stated.

"Fine. But we know about as much about sprites and what they can do as we do demons. He better be able to pull his own weight," Jasmin said. "I'll step out and give him a call; see if he's free to join us."

Torie nodded before taking a lingering look at the sleeping wolf on her couch, and then stole a glance at her worried son.

"It's going to be fine," she said, trying to allay his fears. "Until I get back, I want you to stay inside this house. Fionna will stay with you, and Max will be here as well." She glanced at her two friends, nodding. "Look after Elric for me. When I get back, I'm going to tell you everything that's happened since I've been here."

"You shouldn't do this," said Vera.

Jasmin stared at her. "These women being targeted are your people. We are trying to save more lives and stop a monster. Either help us or don't; but don't tell us what we shouldn't do just because it's something you *won't* do. Either come with us or keep quiet."

Neither of the older women spoke or moved.

"Yeah. Didn't think so," said Jasmin. "Come on, Torie. Let's go find a demon."

Chapter Twelve

They waited outside for Dr. Faun to return to Torie's house. While they had offered to pick him up, he had been adamant that there was no need for that. He arrived in a dark blue sedan with his official medical examiner plates, and pulled up the drive, stopping next to Torie's SUV.

It had taken some work for her to convince Shawn not to wait outside for them. He was stubborn but had finally given in and stomped back inside to sulk. As much as she would have liked his company, Torie knew that having him waiting at her side would have put doubt into her mind as to whether or not she should be leaving him.

And when one was leaving to possibly confront a demon, doubt was the last thing she needed to experience.

They settled into the car, Jasmin in the front seat, Torie in the back, and Dr. Faun pulled carefully away from the house, heading northeast towards the foothills of a mountain range that bordered Singing Falls.

Torie leaned forward. "Dr. Faun," she began, before seeing the look he shot her in the rearview mirror. "Excuse me...Emil...are you familiar with this Devil's Tramping Ground?"

"Not exactly," he replied. "I am new to the area, and therefore not as up-to-date on local lore as I would like. However, I did phone a friend on my way to pick you up and she was nice enough to fill me in on what it was."

Torie didn't say anything at first as she took in Jasmin's reaction to his words. The slight stiffening of her spine as she turned to glance at him, as well as the tiniest of arching in Jasmin's eyebrow told Torie she was wondering just who this "she" was the doctor had phoned.

If the situation they were in weren't so dire, Torie might have found the idea of a jealous Jasmin amusing. But there was nothing amusing about what they were about to face.

"From what I was told, the Devil's Tramping Ground was explained by scientists from the state geological survey teams. They found that there were higher than usual amounts of salt in the soil that made up the circle where the Devil supposedly tread. That salt is what rendered the soil incapable of growing anything," Emil said.

Jasmin looked over her shoulder at Torie, giving her a knowing nod.

"What? Did I miss something?" asked the doctor, not taking his eyes off the road.

"Salt is one of the original magics of the old world, used by the first witches and humans alike to ward off evil and trap spirits," said Jasmin.

"Maybe the original settlers in this area tried it against whatever they thought was plaguing them," added Torie.

"OG magic," said Jasmin. "But if they salted an area enough that it has lasted this long, they must have been up against something very nasty."

Emil didn't respond, but the tightening of his grip on

the steering wheel told the women he was debating whether or not to say something more.

"What is it, Emil?" Torie asked.

He inhaled sharply, glancing into the mirror to briefly lock eyes with her. "Speaking as someone trained in the scientific arts, I can say that salting the earth could indeed have created the problem described. And I would also add that there are various other reasons someone would salt the earth that have nothing whatsoever to do with malevolent spirits."

"I sense a 'but' coming," said Jasmin.

"But the sprite in me knows there are places in the world that have been desecrated by the touch of evil. There are some supernaturals out there that create such darkness, that nature itself will shrink from its touch. And knowing that Singing Falls rests over a confluence of powerful ley lines, I am inclined to believe you are about to confront the latter."

Torie and Jasmin exchanged glances. They had faced death together on many occasions and had always triumphed. Torie knew it wasn't the belief they had in their power that gave them the advantage; rather it was the belief they had in one another.

"Well, this is just reconnaissance," said Torie. "We aren't going to be confronting anything. We just need to get a better idea of what we might be up against."

"So, magical soil samples?" said Dr. Faun, a slight smile spreading across his features.

"Yes! Exactly that. I like that term," said Jasmin.

They continued in silence until the doctor's GPS informed them they had arrived at their destination. Emil eased the car off the road and came to a stop in a large, empty gravel parking lot. The sign that heralded the entrance to the lot read "Heaven's Campground" in bold green lettering on a white background.

"Wait, the Devil's Tramping Ground is…a campsite?" said Torie.

"Not exactly," said Emil. "The locals depend on these mountains to provide tourism dollars; without it, they would be in big trouble. Having it be known that the area is cursed by the Devil wouldn't be good for business. So, they created this campground to make the tourists feel welcome. The area we are after is off an unmarked trail a mile or so up the path. From there, it's a hike to get to the actual Tramping Ground. It's been corded off and marked with signs reading unstable ground and quicksand."

Jasmin stopped in her tracks.

"There isn't any quicksand," Emil said. "It's just something that keeps anyone who ventures too close to the area from wandering farther in. Quicksand is a universal fear and works a lot better than signs saying no trespassing."

Jasmin gave Torie a glance and let out a deep breath before mumbling that she better not get swallowed, before following Emil as he made his way across the gravel. He had a flashlight in one hand; it was small and made of hard plastic with a rubber grip. Despite its size it gave off a powerful beam of light which he shone at the various signs marking the trails with arrows. They were color coded; red, yellow and green, and each color corresponded to a different degree of difficulty and altitude of the path it marked.

"This way," he said, heading into the night.

He had given both Torie and Jasmin a flashlight like his own, and Torie shined hers on the sign marking the path he chose.

Red. Most difficult and steepest.

"Don't worry," he said over his shoulder, almost as if he had read her mind. "The trail doesn't get bad until after the point where we break off. This shouldn't be too hard at all for either of you."

Jasmin huffed. "A teleportation spell would make this a lot easier you know."

Emil stopped and turned to face them. "True. But the use of magic could very well alert whoever, or whatever, dwells in here. Right now, you have the advantage of surprise. Do you want to give that up?"

Torie frowned. "No. We don't. Don't worry about us; we'll be fine."

He smiled and turned, continuing forward.

"So, how do you know where we go to find this place?" Jasmin asked.

"As I said, my friend is well acquainted with the area. She told me exactly where to go to get there."

"Maybe we should have invited her along," said Torie.

"I tried. She said she'd rather trek into hell itself than visit this place," the sprite replied over his shoulder.

Torie felt Jasmin's eyes burrow into the back of her head as they closed the gap between them and their guide. For a moment, Torie wished they had brought Max with them. Or even Fionna. Having someone along who could see in the dark and hear the things they couldn't, would have come in very handy just then.

As hard as it was, she resisted the urge to cast a sliver of magic into the woods around her, just to make sure nothing was shadowing them. But what Emil had explained made sense. Besides, they were hiking along a main trail in what was apparently a very popular spot. How much danger could they really be in?

She pushed aside any thoughts of things that might go

bump in the night, and instead focused on her surroundings. The moon wasn't quite full, but between that and the play of their flashlights, she could see that it was a truly beautiful area. She loved the crispness of the night air in the mountains. The days could be hot, but the nights were perfect. A cooling mist made its way down from the top of the mountain, creating just the right amount of chill on her skin. The smell of old growth, stone, and decaying brush brought to mind images of an old hay barn at a petting zoo she used to visit as a child. That, combined with the sound of——

She stopped, looking around.

That was what was missing. At some point during their hike, the normal sounds of the woods had stopped. It was eerily silent as Emil stopped. The trail they were on veered off to the right, yet he shined his light straight ahead, into the denser forestry.

"We need to go through here. It will be a little trickier, so watch your footing. But the Tramping Ground should be about a mile straight ahead," he said.

They hadn't gone twenty steps when Torie began to feel a little lightheaded. She glanced at Jasmin and could tell her friend was feeling it as well.

"What is that?" she asked.

"It's the same feeling Fionna and Max described," Jasmin answered. "Maybe it's not just shifters that are affected."

The thought that something could be playing havoc with their magic caused Torie's stomach to knot. She had to stop briefly to fight against the foreign feeling creeping into her body. Taking a deep breath, she pushed the urge to run away from her mind.

"You feel that as well?" said Jasmin. "Something just

triggered our fight or flight response; and it feels like flight is winning." She looked over at Emil who was regarding the two witches with concern. "How are you feeling, Emil?"

His brow furrowed slightly. "Honestly, I'm not getting whatever it is that is impacting the two of you. Sprites are grounded in the earth. The closer we get, the more of a disconnect I feel with mother nature; but that's about it. There is no physical discomfort for me. Should we head back?"

"We've come this far," said Jasmin, "we might as well keep going. I want to see this pit for myself; plus, I'm starting to feel a little better."

Torie nodded. "Same here. Whatever that was, it's passing."

Emil turned without a word and pushed on. Soon, he led them through the last line of dense growth before stepping into a clearing. Pointing his light ahead, he turned to the witches.

"There. That's it; straight ahead."

Torie and Jasmin stepped around him, glaring at the barren area that lay in the center of the clearing. It was just as Fionna described; a circular worn-down path with no vegetation growing around it. It felt ominous, even to Torie.

She squinted in the dim light. "There is something lying in the circle," she whispered.

She heard Jasmin gasp at the same time she realized what she was looking at. It wasn't a *something* in the circle; but rather, a *someone.*

Or to be more precise, multiple someones. There were bodies strewn about the area, though how many they couldn't tell.

"My God," said Emil. "Those poor people."

Before either Torie or Jasmin could stop him, he was

running forward, headed towards the bodies. For a man of indeterminate age, he covered the ground far quicker than the women would have guessed him capable of. Try as they might to keep up, he pulled away effortlessly and made it to the spot called the Devil's Tramping Ground well before either of them.

They made their way to him, huffing, hands on hips trying to stave off the pinching in their sides.

"Emil, you...you shouldn't just run off like that," Torie said. "We don't know what killed these people——"

"They aren't dead," he said, not taking his eyes off the bodies. "I know death; I can sense it from far away. These young women are all still alive."

A sound drifted across the barren circle that raised the hair on the back of their necks. It was a huffing sound, followed by the stench of fetid breath. Together, they turned to see the same large bear Max and Elric had chased out of town. It was immense, with mammoth paws that raked the ground before it. Eyes that glowed with green energy narrowed at them.

In its jaws, it held the body of yet another young woman, hanging limp, her clothing snagged on inches-long, razor-sharp teeth.

The bear dropped the woman to the side before turning to face the witches. Then, with a roar that split the night, it charged.

Chapter Thirteen

Head lowered, the shaggy beast raced at them, green eyes hissing eldritch steam and spittle flying from its open mouth as it closed the distance between them.

Jasmin threw a glowing shield up before them at the last moment, just as Torie grabbed Emil and pushed him aside, knocking him to the ground behind her as she raised her own hands, glowing with her magic. Torie spun to face the creature, throwing her own magic into the protective barrier.

The shield shimmered and held as the beast collided with it, snarling and clawing. Emil scrambled to his feet; eyes wide in terror. The great shifter was relentless, pounding against the barrier with its massive body, trying to break through. Finally, with a desperate push, it breached the shield and lunged at Emil, teeth bared.

He fell backward as the bear dropped on top of him, its great, wet maw inches from closing on his head. Emil closed his eyes, choosing not to look death in the face, and waited for the snap that would most likely sever his head from his body.

It was a snap that didn't come. And when he opened one eye to peek, he saw the bear's mouth held firmly closed by a ghostly blue muzzle. He glanced aside and saw Torie standing there, hands glowing with the same blue magic, struggling against the bear's strength as it sought to free itself of the constraints she had cast around its jaws.

Still in shock, Emil felt a jolt shoot through his body, a surprising shock, but not terribly unpleasant. A yellow light surrounded him, solidifying, and pulling him away from the bear's reach. Jasmin had cast a glowing spell that propelled the sprite away from them, throwing him out of harm's way as she closed in on the shifter from behind.

Sensing her approach, the bear wheeled with surprising speed. With a swipe of its great paw, it broke through Torie's muzzle and lowered its massive head at Jasmin. It charged, and she dove to one side, barely escaping the claws that raked the air where she had been standing only seconds before. Hitting the ground, she stabbed both hands into the earth as she whispered an incantation into the night.

The ground around her rumbled as she called for sleeping vegetation to spring forth and restrain the creature.

Only nothing happened. The rumble stopped, and the look of shock on her face spurred the monster on to attack her yet again.

Before he could land on her, Torie acted, calling on her magic to generate more restraints, this time in the form of glowing chains. She cast them about the beast, driving the free ends into the earth to fasten him in place. The shifter roared in anger and threw its bulk against the chains.

Looking on in shock, Torie watched as her construct began to weaken. Blackness crept from the earth into her chains, degrading the magic within. Soon, they crumbled, breaking into a million pieces and falling away from the bear in a shower of fragmented black light.

Before it could attack, Jasmin hit the creature with a beam of pure magic, stabbing deep into the bear's side. It howled in pain, turning its attention to Jasmin as she circled around for another strike. Taking a cue from her friend, Torie called up a ball of fire and cast it at the shifter, engulfing its form in flames. Jasmin whirled, sending three glowing daggers of power flying at the beast. They struck, burying themselves in his back.

Jasmin closed her fist in the air, then opened it quickly and yanked her arm backwards. The daggers followed her commands and ripped themselves out of the bear's hide, bringing bits of muscle and fur with it. The shifter howled once more before dropping to all fours. Its head swung back and forth from Torie to Jasmin as it considered its chances against the two powerful witches.

While the women could not read its thoughts, it must have decided discretion was the better part of valor as it surged forward, turning to run away from the witches. Leaping over the bodies of the young women, it disappeared into the night, the sound of its heavy footfall echoing throughout the darkness long after it had vanished from sight.

Torie turned to start after it, but Jasmin placed a hand on her arm in restraint.

"No, let it go. We have bigger worries here," she said, indicating the women around them.

Emil ran up to them, just as Torie cast a ball of softly glowing light into the air. It illuminated the bodies around them, and Torie was able to make out that they were breathing, though very shallowly.

"Can you do something for them?" she asked, turning to Emil.

The sprite looked at the women, his eyes darting from one to the other. There was a total of five, including the most recent addition the bear had dropped.

"I...I don't know how much help I will be. I'm a medical examiner; I'm used to working on dead things. These women are...very much alive." He bent to study the first, carefully turning her over and leaning in to place his ear near her mouth. "Her respiratory rate is very low, pulse is thready, and her skin is clammy to the touch. It's almost like they are in some form of shock."

Jasmin took out her phone and held it aloft. "And of course, no signal here."

"Can you generate some fire to keep them warm?" said Emil. "That will help. But we need to get some medics and ambulances up here soon, or they may not make it."

Torie immediately called up a sizzling ball of fire and placed it on the ground, bathing them in heat and additional light. Almost immediately, it sputtered, the flames turning black and flickering until they finally faded away.

Torie looked at Jasmin. "It's the ground here. It has to be. That's why our magic kept failing when we were fighting that bear shifter. This place is weakening us."

Jasmin's eyes grew wide as she considered her words. She turned to Emil. "Maybe they aren't in shock. Could this ground we are standing on be doing something to them? Infecting them somehow?"

"It's possible. Let's get them out of this and see."

Both Jasmin and Torie's eyes began to glow as they held their hands out. Carefully, they levitated the five bodies into the air and gently floated them into the clearing, away from the patch of dead ground.

"I definitely feel better," said Jasmin. "Whatever that ground is, it was leeching the strength from us. But why wasn't it hurting the shifter as well?"

"We'll worry about that later," Torie said. "First, we need to make sure these women are okay."

Emil was already attending to one. He looked up, eyes wide and hopeful. "Her vitals are already starting to stabilize. Whatever was done to them, it seems like they're starting to snap out of it."

A few moans began to escape the lips of some of the women as they slowly came around. They were all too weak to move, but at least they were regaining consciousness.

"They still need to be checked out," said Emil. "The sooner the better."

"We still can't get any signal out here," said Jasmin, checking her phone once again.

"Maybe we don't have to," Torie said.

She lifted her head, holding her arms out to her side as she whispered an incantation.

"Spirits of the moon, hear my plea,
and carry my words, to the one I need."

The air shimmered as her spell took shape and amplified her words, carrying them across the night sky.

"Fionna. We need ambulances and medical services. Heaven's Campground," she whispered into the air.

"Do you think your friend will be able to receive that?" enquired Emil.

"I have a natural rapport with shifters and can communicate with them telepathically, but only when they are in their animal forms. I've never tried it with any other than

Elric when they are in human form. Let's hope it works with Fionna."

"Interesting," he replied, moving to yet another of the women to examine.

"We still need to get them to the campground parking lot," said Jasmin. "Together, without that pit working against us, we should be able to levitate them."

The moans of the women increased as they slowly began to sit up, shaking their heads. Some held their heads in their hands, while others rubbed at their throats. All seemed more than a little shaken and confused.

"They need fluids. Definitely dehydrated," said Emil. "I think they've been out here for some time."

Torie started to answer but then stopped, her body going rigid. Her head snapped around and she stared into the distant darkness. Magic flared to life around her as she stood ramrod stiff.

In response, Jasmin called up her own power, moving to stand next to her friend. "Torie, what is it?"

"I don't know," she whispered, not taking her eyes off the undergrowth. "There's something…out there. Watching us."

"Maybe that bear shifter circled back around," Emil said. He closed his eyes, cocking his head to one side. "I don't hear or smell anything."

Torie narrowed her eyes before letting her magic slowly die down. "Whatever that was, it wasn't a shifter. We need to get these women away from here." She looked to Jasmin, questioningly. "I don't know if they are human or supernatural, but we are going to have to risk revealing our powers to them."

Jasmin nodded as she stepped back. She gestured at the ground, whispering to the undergrowth around her.

"Without that darned pit to interfere, I can feel nature responding to me." With that, she gestured into the air, her fingers crossing and uncrossing in complicated hex formations meant to invoke earth magic.

The vines twisted beneath them until they formed a long, green and brown sled; one that Jasmin's magic would enable her to drive, carrying the women out of the wooded area and back to the parking lot.

"Get them onboard and let's get out of here," she said.

Emil nodded, turning to help Torie rally the women enough to stumble onto the sled. "Now that is some serious magic. Can you do that?"

"I'm not as good with earth magic as Jasmin is. If I tried that, it might work, but it would just as likely pull trees out of the ground by their roots. I'm more of a sledgehammer witch, whereas Jasmin is like a skilled surgeon."

Her voice trailed off. She loved being a witch, but sometimes felt like she would never possess the finer skills that Jasmin, and from what she had heard, her mother, possessed.

Emil offered a quick smile. "That's alright. There are plenty of times when a sledgehammer is called for to get certain jobs done."

"Hey, if y'all are done chit-chatting, can we move now?" came Jasmin's voice. She was standing at the front of the sled, the glow of her eyes matching the faint nimbus of light that imbued the vines she conjured to hold the five women.

Torie marveled at her friend and nodded for Emil to follow closely. She took one last look behind them and then watched as Jasmin bade the sled to move forward through the forest undergrowth. Had it not been such an effortless manner of transport, it might have been creepy. The path before them was in constant motion with vines and roots reaching up to pass the sled along, and then. receding back into the earth once their job was done.

Looking back, Torie could see no signs that they had ever passed; the woodland retained its wild, untouched appearance.

Good.

It ensured that no one would stumble onto anything that could resemble a path and take it to the Tramping Ground. Thinking back on that pit, she felt a chill race up her spine.

Every instinct she had told her that whoever, or whatever, had created that was older and darker than anything they had ever encountered. On a whim, she snaked a bit of magic into the woods behind them, sending a tiny thread of power trailing out.

Something touched it; tugging at it like an insect might set off the trip line in a spider's web. Something that reeked of evil and darkness. But then, just as quickly as contact was made, it was gone.

Torie nodded slowly in understanding. Whatever had taken up residence in these woods was far too dangerous to live. There were so many questions going on in her life right now, questions she didn't have the answers to.

But destroying this darkness was something she knew had to be done. She had friends and family that depended on her, and she wasn't about to let them down. One way or another, she and this demon were on a collision course.

Her eyes blazed in the darkness as she considered what needed to be done. She knew Jasmin might not approve, but it was time to bring out the big guns.

Emil was right. Being a sledgehammer was needed at times.

Chapter Fourteen

"Are you sure about this?" Jasmin asked. "I mean…it's a lot."

Torie exhaled slowly, weighing her words carefully. "This is what I always had in mind when I built that house, remember? I wanted it to be a safe haven for any in need. And right now, as far as I can see, these young women are very much in need."

Once they had arrived at the parking lot, it wasn't long before the wail of the ambulances gave way to flashing lights and a cacophony of near chaos as multiple units arrived on the scene. A car pulled in with a screech, sending tiny bits of gravel flying into the air. Fionna and Glen jumped out, rushing to their friends.

"Heads up, I told them there must have been some kind of gas leak and there were multiple injuries reported," said Fionna.

"Good thinking," Jasmin said approvingly.

Glen had her medical bag in hand as she turned to face Emil. "Anything in particular I need to know? I know these guys that responded to the call. They can be trusted with secrets if need be."

Emil shook his head. "As far as I can tell they are all human. No signs of head trauma, but they seem to be in shock; definitely in need of hydration."

Glen nodded and rushed off to help the paramedics assess the women.

"The ones recovered enough to talk have no idea where they are or how they got here," Emil said.

"Erin said the same thing at the store. She doesn't remember the shifter attacking," said Jasmin.

"But she knew the Fate sisters," said Torie. "What are the odds that these women will recognize them as well?"

They spent the next hour going from unit to unit as the women were examined. Luckily, Glen was able to guide the paramedics into agreeing that the women did not need hospital stays for their treatment, and the lone police officer who responded to the call was someone Max had contacted in his force and asked to run interference for the rest of the department, keeping them away.

He was a leopard shifter named Terrance and had only been in Singing Falls for a month. He looked nervous as Torie approached him. He blinked hard at her, but then nodded as he seemed to recognize who she was.

"Hello, ma'am," he said. "Max sent me. You must be Torie. He said you and your friends would make the call as to what I was to do up here."

He looked around, unsure what to make of the scene. Torie searched her memory for any mention of him from Max but couldn't quite place the man. It wasn't like Max to entrust something like this to a newbie, but then she remembered that the wolf was guarding her guests, and that meant Elric had yet to recover. She was thankful Max had taken her requests to watch over everyone seriously, so the least she could do was make this as painless as possible for the newbie.

"Don't worry, we pretty much have this under control. The biggest thing is keeping it quiet; we don't need something like this hitting the media. Did you hear anything on the police scanner about this coming in?"

He shook his head. "No, ma'am. Not a peep. Even the paramedics kept the call quiet."

She was nodding. This would make keeping a lid on things a lot easier. Singing Falls might be a supernatural community, but it was also a small town; and if there was one thing small towns excelled at, it was spreading gossip.

This was a town that had survived a vampire serial killer, an attack by a golem, a homicidal hunter, and a murderous Chimera; it had seen its fair share of horrors, and the last thing Torie wanted was for the community to get in an uproar once again because something might be coming to kill everyone.

She wasn't going to allow that to happen. So that meant keeping a lid on everything that was happening. Another reason to have all the women stay at her house. Under one roof, she could not only protect them, but also control the narrative so as not to frighten the townsfolk.

"We need to get everyone back to the house as soon as possible," she said as Jasmin walked up. "We can take two in Emil's car, and Glen and Fionna can drive the rest." She looked around, her eyes squinting into the darkness once again. "Something was following us."

Jasmin nodded slightly. "I thought so. Maybe it was the bear shifter?"

"I don't think so. Whatever it was, it evaded my magic pretty easily."

"We will deal with it when the time is right. But after we learn more about it; and on our terms."

Torie couldn't argue with that. There were so many questions that needed answering. But there would be time for that later. First things first. She looked over at Glen and Emil, watching as they worked with the paramedics.

Emil nodded, giving her a thumbs up, and together, they ushered the women into their cars and pulled out of Heaven's Campground.

Chapter Fifteen

Max was pacing back and forth inside the great room when they returned to the house. He threw himself at the witches as soon as they opened the door.

"What did you find out? Terrance told me you had a run in with the same bear shifter Elric and I fought. Is that true? Are you okay? He would never forgive me if you were hurt." His questions came at them rapid fire; so quickly that his words nearly tripped over themselves getting out of his mouth.

He looked past her shoulder, his eyes focusing on the women making their way up the sidewalk towards them. They looked exhausted; dirty, clothes tattered, and more than a couple had bruises and cuts on their faces. His gaze softened and he stepped aside as Torie smiled, beckoning them inside.

"I'll get some water on for tea," he said softly, heading for the kitchen. "I'll put out some food as well."

"Thank you," Torie said, softly. She reached for him before he had disappeared from view. "How's Elric?"

Max smiled softly. "He's fine. He even moved upstairs to the bedroom. When one of us is healing to the degree he is, we crave sleep more than anything. But he's going to be fine."

Torie sighed, her eyes thanking him more than any words she could have mustered. She eased the women into the great room, followed by Fionna, Glen and Emil. Each woman stopped, looking around the spacious, well-appointed room.

"It's okay," Torie said, gesturing towards the furniture. "Trust me, you aren't going to hurt anything. It's all wash and wear so please...have a seat." It wasn't wash and wear, but she made a mental note to have the fabric swapped out with something a little less fussy to deal with.

Just as everyone was settling down, Shawn rushed into the room and threw his arms around his mother. Torie fought back tears as she hugged him, nearly overcome by his emotional state.

"There, see...I told you I would be back. And look, I brought some more company." She continued to pat his back until he finally looked around the room. "I think it might be nice if everyone introduced themselves. It seems like we might be here for a while."

While Glen had tended to as many of the women as possible at the parking lot, she still made the rounds, crouching before each, speaking softly to them, and offering them aspirin from her kit as well as applying more antibiotic creams to cuts.

"That's Glen; she's our Florence Nightingale. This is Dr. Emil Faun, whom you've also met." She motioned towards the sprite standing in the doorway. "This is Jasmin, that's my son Shawn, and the big gruffy guy who opened the door is Max; he's our town sheriff. I'm Torie, and this is my house. But as long as you're here, it's your home too. We are all here to help you."

"Can I ask, do all of you know one another?" questioned Jasmin.

The women looked around, studying one another before shaking their heads.

"I don't recognize anyone. My name is Jane and, honestly, I'm not even sure how I ended up in the woods. It's all very foggy. The last thing I remember was buying a bus ticket to Singing Falls, but I don't know why. I just knew I had to come here," said one of the women. She was the last one the bear shifter had brought into the Devil's Tramping Ground before the fight with Torie and Jasmin. The back of the leather jacket she was wearing had large gashes taken out of it where the shifter had carried her in its jaws.

All the women murmured in agreement.

Movement in the periphery of her vision caught Torie's attention and she turned just as Erin was walking slowly into the great room, her eyes trained on the women. She stopped, her gaze moving slowly from one to the next.

"Erin, do you know any of these women?" asked Torie.

Slowly, Erin nodded in response. "Yes. I do...or rather they are all familiar to me. But I don't know from where or when."

"Well, that's because these are your sisters." It was Vera's voice as she and her sister appeared behind Erin, stepping into the room. "You recognize them because you share a similar destiny. However, for their own protection, none of them have been introduced to the others. They are all from different regions. That way, no one can be compelled to reveal the location of another."

When they stepped into the room, all the women stood, transfixed by the sight of the older Fates.

The sisters nodded to each of them.

"Welcome, Jane, Cassie, Myra, Judith, and Sharon. You are here because circumstances dictated that you be," said Corin, her tone filled with the promise of things yet to be revealed.

"How…how do I know you?" asked the one Corin had called Cassie. "I've never seen you before, and yet, I have."

More murmurs of agreement spread throughout the space as the two older sisters smiled. Vera held up a hand and motioned for them to have a seat. Silence slowly settled over the room as Max walked back in carrying an impressively large tray overflowing with sandwiches cut into fours in one hand, and a second tray laden with bottled water in the other. He placed them both on the large coffee table near the couches and stepped back, beckoning the women to help themselves.

They seemed immediately distrustful, casting sideways glances at him.

"Is he…?" began the woman introduced as Judith.

Another younger woman nodded. Her name was Sharon and she squinted hard at Max. "He's a monster of some kind…I can see it!"

Before the rest could join in the clamor, Corin raised both hands. "Ladies, calm down. Max isn't a monster; he's a werewolf. Your senses are sharp, but not yet attuned to the supernatural around you. Give it time."

While it was obvious her words were meant to assuage their feelings of distrust, they had quite the opposite effect as the women screamed when Max took a step forward, clambering back on the various pieces of furniture on which they sat, while one of them hastily reached for a bottle of water and held it over her head like a club.

"No, it's okay, don't be afraid," said Fionna, stepping forward. "Look, I'm a shifter too." With that, the air shimmered briefly around her as she shed her human form, dropping to the ground as a squirrel and then reappearing as human.

"Yes, and Torie and I are witches," said Jasmin. She held out her hand, palm up, and conjured a ball of light that transformed into a shimmering, translucent horse that galloped in place before disappearing in a tiny shower of light.

"You're in a town filled with supernaturals," added Torie. "And the fact that you were called here tells me there may be more to the lot of you than meets the eye."

A meow reached their ears as Leo entered the room, rushing to rub against Torie's legs, begging her to lift him.

"And this," she said, reaching down, "Is my dragon, Leo."

The magic surrounding the cat disappeared, revealing Leo in his true form as he nuzzled against Torie, his wings shimmering in the light.

Torie looked at Jasmin with surprise. "And I didn't just do that. The spell cloaking him just dropped away."

Shawn jumped aside; eyes wide at the sight of the baby dragon purring contentedly in his mother's arms. "What the heck, Mom? That thing was curled up on my bed!"

"Oh hush. That thing saved our lives once. And if he's stayed on your bed, he knows what you mean to me and is protecting you as well," Torie replied.

In response to her words, Leo lifted out of her arms and hovered over to land on Shawn's shoulder, puffing out a light stream of smoke as he rubbed his snout against the boy's hair. Shawn opened his mouth to speak, but instead, reached up a hand to scratch at the little dragon.

The sheer cuteness of it all nearly won the women over, but still their eyes flitted around the room, settling on the doctor who had cared for them.

"I am a sprite," Emil said, his voice as low and non-threatening as he could make it. "I'm just a magical wood-land creature who specializes in death."

They shrieked and jumped back yet again, this time a second grabbed a bottle of water for protection.

"Okay, everyone calm down," said Vera, her voice ringing out through the large room. "All of you sit down, now. You're going to be exposed to far worse than this I fear, so you may as well get used to it."

As one, the women all returned to their seats. Torie noticed that Erin followed suit, claiming a spot in one of the large wing-backed chairs at the same time.

"There is no danger here, for any of you," she contin-ued. "These witches and wolves and their friends are here to protect you. And trust me, right now, you need that protec-tion." Once she had all eyes on her, she continued, looking toward her sister and giving a nod of encouragement.

Corin stepped forward, raising both hands in the air. She closed her eyes, and when she opened them, the orbs had become solid gray. A shimmer moved through the air from her to the women, settling around their heads before disappearing.

In response, their eyes flashed briefly and when it cleared, they seemed far more focused and relaxed.

"There. Now isn't that better?" asked Vera, her lips turning upward.

"Are all these women your disciples?" asked Jasmin.

Vera nodded. "They are the last. There are seven disciples of the Fates. These women, plus Erin, are the last. The seventh…well, you know what happened to her."

Corin turned to Torie. "Thank you. For opening your home to us, and for saving these children. Because of you, we might just survive this."

Torie felt heat rise in her face. She had never been good with accepting compliments; especially not one of this magnitude. Hiding her blush, she nodded, before raising another question.

"What exactly is it the demon wants with these women? How does the bear shifter fit in, and why was he placing them in the pit like that?"

Vera shrugged her shoulders. "The demon, like all supernaturals of its status, have representatives in this world. They utilize other beings to do their bidding in certain situations. The reasons vary; it could be because it sees some work as beneath it, a waste of time."

"Or it could be because it has not yet reached its full potential. Crossing into this world from the dark dimensions takes a lot out of them. He could still be recovering," said Corin.

Jasmin's head snapped around. "So, you mean it might be vulnerable right now?"

Torie was nodding. "That would explain why it didn't come to the aid of the bear shifter."

Max squinted at the witches. "Uh-uh. No. I know what you're thinking and you're not going back out there again."

"I would agree," said Vera before either Torie or Jasmin could respond to the wolf. "Even a weakened Nerian is more than a match for two hex witches. Perhaps you should consider convening your coven. Combine all of your powers."

Torie and Jasmin gave her a questioning look.

"We don't have a coven," Jasmin said. "We are the only two hex witches that I know of on the eastern seaboard."

Vera's eyes widened. "Nonsense. We have sensed the presence of many hex witches at work in this town. We assumed you were part of a much larger coven."

Torie threw Jasmin a look. Her friend gave her a slight shake of her head, eyes filled with the same questions as Torie's.

If there were other hex witches in the area, surely they would know, right? The Fate sisters had to be sensing something else. There was no way a coven of witches could be operating inside Singing Falls and Torie and Jasmin not know.

Torie made a mental note to ask Jasmin just how many witches made up a coven. And Vera had said she felt *many* hex witches around them…wouldn't that make them a coven?

"Well, if this is the case," said Corin, concern rising in her voice, "then perhaps my sister and I have made a grave mistake. You see, we came here not only seeking the help of a powerful coven of hex witches, Torie Bliss; but we have also come to recruit you. We want you to replace our fallen sister. We want you to become the next Fate."

Chapter Sixteen

Torie blinked rapidly while staring at the two sisters, who now seemed to be beside themselves in exasperation and were engaged in a fast-paced, hushed-tone conversation in one another's ears.

"Okay, hold up," said Jasmin, raising both hands for attention, "can you guys speak one at a time and loud enough for us to hear? Because for one thing, it's just plain manners, and for another…Torie isn't going anywhere." The steel-hard look in her eyes told the room that her entire statement had come down to the hard emphasis she placed on the last four words she had spoken.

She stepped forward, leveling the sisters with her gaze.

Jasmin's eyes blazed yellow. "You're still hiding something. Tell us everything," she said to the sisters. Then, turning to Fionna. "Listen to their heartbeats. Tell me if they're lying."

The shifter nodded gravely and closed her eyes, tilting her head to one side in the direction of the Fates as she sank deep into her senses. She cast aside the steady staccato drum of Max's heart, Torie's light pitter as she focused on her breathing, and Jasmin's calm and steady, metronome-like rhythm. Instead, she focused on the frantic, uneven heartbeats of the two sisters, listening closely for any spikes that might coincide with an untruth.

The elderly women looked at one another, each rubbing her hands together, trying unsuccessfully to quell nervous energy.

"Fine, fine," said Corin throwing up her hands. "What we said was true. We did come here looking for your protection. It's true that we cannot engage in battle on this plane…only observe outcomes."

"And influence them?" Torie asked.

A slight pause and then Corin nodded her head. "We can play a part in the outcome, depending on the circumstances. But if you think we would manipulate you into making a decision about joining us, I can assure you that would never happen."

Jasmin glanced at Fionna, who nodded her head in response.

"Why do I feel like there's a 'but' coming?" inquired Jasmin.

Vera took a deep breath. "However, we can admit that we were on our way here to recruit you *before* the demon attacked our disciples. We had no idea they were in danger; we would have never summoned them had we known."

"What do you mean you had no idea?" said Max. It was the first time the big wolf had spoken, and the Fate's words had piqued his curiosity. "Why are they here if not for protection?"

"Well, we were going to offer them to your coven as way of…payment for you," Corin mumbled.

No one said a word. It felt like breath itself had been suspended in the room.

Then, all Jasmin broke loose.

"Are you saying you brought these women here to...to trade them or sell them in exchange for another human being?" she exclaimed, hands clenched as her eyes blazed furiously. The air around her rippled with the power of the anger coursing through her. The lamps and knick-knacks arranged throughout the space trembled in cadence with the pulse of magic.

The air around her felt like it was charged with electricity, causing the hairs on Torie's arms to stand on edge.

"Jas...it's okay," she said, reaching for her friend.

"The heck it is. They are treating these women like chattel; like something they own that can just be thrown aside when they see fit," Jasmin replied. Her voice was dark and filled with magic.

The two sisters seemed confused by Jasmin's sudden outburst.

"No, you don't understand," said Corin. "This is what the disciples are for. From time immemorial until now, we raise, care for and train these disciples for this very moment. When a Fate dies, her replacement is always the most powerful witch from that generation."

"In this case, we were led to you to be her replacement," said Vera. "But I assure you, we value these young women as highly as we would any life form."

"So, the reason they are here...the reason that woman was killed; was because of me?" asked Torie, her voice constricting.

"The demon that killed our sister knows that we are at the time of a calling——that's what it is to replace a fallen Fate——it makes sense that it would be here to prevent that from happening. Which is why the sooner all is done, the better," said Corin.

Jasmin bristled, the air thrumming again. "There you go again. Speaking like it's a done deal...this disgusting trade, or whatever it is."

"Forgive me. I misspoke," said Corin. "But no one who has ever been called has failed to join the sisterhood..."

Fionna stiffened. "No. Something about that was off."

Jasmin stared at the sisters. "Care to clarify?"

"Well...the calling is so rare. The only ones who have not joined were prevented in doing so by...things out of their control," said Vera.

"Such as?" said Jasmin.

The sisters exchanged looks. Finally, Corin shrugged.

"Well, some died in making the transition from this world to ours...but that is exceedingly rare," Vera said. Then she turned her attention to Torie. "And it most certainly would not happen with you, not with your lineage and power."

Her sister snapped a look that froze Vera in place.

"What lineage? What are you talking about?" Torie asked.

"Forgive us," said Corin. "My sister and I have said too much already."

"Don't stop now, tell us what you know about my lineage," Torie demanded.

Corin shook her head. "You have to understand; the Fates see everything; what was, what is and, at times, what has yet to come. But there are certain things we cannot reveal; in order to maintain certain balances. All things will be revealed, but not until the time is right. For both our sakes, please don't ask us any more on that subject."

Jasmin's eyes narrowed as she regarded the sisters. "So

then are you saying it is a forgone conclusion that Torie will be joining you? Can you at least tell us that much?"

Corin shook her head. "We can only ask; but we can't influence your decision. But I will say that...your presence among the Fates is foretold. But exactly how? That's still a little cloudy, even for us." She regarded Torie with her head cocked slightly to one side.

Max had resumed his pacing around the room, and Shawn hadn't taken his eyes off his mother. She watched her son, unable to read the emotions behind the stoic mask he was projecting. She could only imagine what the conversation was triggering in the young man. Surely, all this talk of abandonment had brought up memories of his father.

Even when his father had been in the picture, he had been far more focused on growing his business than his family. But still, he had been a physical presence in the house for the majority of Shawn's young life. Though his walking out on her had ended up being the best thing that had ever happened, she had been bitter at the time. The only saving grace she saw was that he did it when their son was heading off to college. At least Shawn wouldn't have to spend time in a home living with the ghosts of familial memories.

The two of them had always had a special bond, and it seemed to have grown even stronger after her divorce and subsequent move to Singing Falls. She wanted to ask her son what was going through his mind but knew it wasn't the right time for that. Was he thinking she was going to abandon him as well?

She didn't want that seed taking root in his mind and knew she had to put a stop to it before it could be planted.

"Well, thank you for the offer, but I'm not going anywhere," she said, lifting her chin in defiance. "I've built a home here in Singing Falls. I have a son who needs me; and I need him. I have my friends here...and more." Her thoughts drifted to Elric, still recovering from his horrific wounds. "I don't know what your visions are telling you, but from the moment I set foot in this town, I knew beyond a shadow of a doubt that this is where I belong. And I'm not leaving."

She walked over to her son and gave his hand a squeeze. He trembled in response, and she could feel the waves of relief flowing from the young man.

She caught Jasmin's eye and nodded to her in acknowledgement.

"So. Now that we have that out of the way. What are our next steps? Why would the demon have been gathering these women? And for that matter, how much danger are they still in?" Torie asked.

Corin cleared her throat before speaking up. "They are still in considerable danger. Nerian wants them for a singular purpose; to find out where the new Fate is, so he can destroy that person before they join us."

"By gathering our disciples in his Tramping Grounds, he would have been able to utilize their inherent psychic energy to *see* the coven they were meant for. From there, it would have just been a matter of determining who among that coven was the most likely to ascend to Fatehood. Or he would have simply destroyed the entire coven. Once the demon is assured all hope of us returning to our full power is lost, it would have taken its time hunting the two of us down and killing us. Thus, eliminating the last obstacle that could prevent his master's ascension to full power in this world," said Corin.

"And once that happens?" asked Fionna.

"Say goodbye to your cute little life in the mountains

here," said Vera. "Everything will slowly fall under his domain. He will unleash hell on earth, and it will start with this town."

Torie shivered, hugging herself as she contemplated their words. "So being here places these women in danger for no reason. Why not simply let them return to their lives; wherever they may have come from?"

Vera shook her head. "It's not that simple. As we said, they are still our eyes and ears in the mortal plane. Nerian is aware of them now. Coven or no, he will still hunt them. He will use anything he can to continue to cripple us. If he can't use them to ferret out the next Fate, he will kill them; simply because he knows it will hurt us."

"Why not train one of them to become your next Fate?" asked Fionna.

"Because you can't train a Fate," said Corin. "It is a part of the natural order of gifts that a person either has or they don't. Under normal circumstances, a disciple has the potential to ascend. But these are not normal circumstances. If we are under attack from dark forces, we need someone with seasoned power to join us."

Jasmin was clearly rankled by the conversation but held her tongue as she began to pace back and forth as well.

"So, this brings us back to our next move. What do we do? Just wait around or take the fight to this Nerian demon thing while he's maybe still a bit weak?" she said.

"You aren't a match for it," stated Vera. "You'll both die."

"Why would there only be the two of them?" asked Fionna. "Torie said it; we are a family. Me, Max, Elric... and I'm sure we can gather a few more of the more powerful shifters in town. Could this demon stand against all of us?"

Emil cleared his throat. "I'm in as well. Not sure what I can do, but…I've fallen hard for this little town since I've been here. I'll fight for it as well."

Torie looked around the room at friends old and new and could barely blink back the tears that threatened to leak from her eyes. Their words reinforced what she already knew; this was her family, and she would fight to the bitter end to protect them.

Vera's head whipped around, her eyes locking in on Torie's at that very moment. For a second, Torie thought she felt something crawl over her mind; a slight tickle that brushed her thoughts before disappearing.

Just then, Max's phone rang, and he stepped out to take the call. He was back in a matter of seconds.

"Looks like we don't have to wait too long for that next move," he said. "That was Terrance. They just received an anonymous call saying there was a disturbance at one of the shops on Main Street. And a possible body on site as well."

He stared hard at his friends in the room.

"What is it?" asked Jasmin.

"The address he gave. It's the bakery you guys are opening."

Chapter Seventeen

"Let me go in first," said Max, motioning for Terrance to follow him.

Torie started to ignore him but stopped as she remembered her promise to Shawn. Before leaving the house, she had assured him she wouldn't take any unnecessary risks. So, she waited, standing behind Max's black police SUV and straining to peek around the large vehicle to catch a glimpse of what was going on inside the storefront she was currently renovating with Fionna and Jasmin.

It was intended to be both her escape and a way to give back to the town. It was where she had first met her new family and they welcomed her with open arms. It was the site of so many firsts for her, and she had hopes that it would be the same for many more generations of Singing Falls citizens to come. Working together, she and Jasmin had set up a trust that would keep the new bakery-slash-coffee-shop open long after they were gone.

Of course, that would mean they would have to survive a demon's wrath and whatever else might get thrown their way. Sometimes, she envied her old blinders-wearing self who saw the world through emerald-tinted glasses.

No.

That wasn't true. That Torie was gone and would not be coming back. Dwelling on the past wouldn't change the path she was on now. And what was happening right there, in front of her and her friends, was all that mattered.

She fidgeted, anxious for Max to come out and tell them it was okay to enter the building. Jasmin's hand on her shoulder calmed her nerves, helping her balance her rapid breathing and regain some semblance of control over her body.

What was in fact minutes, felt like hours; but finally, Max and Terrance walked out of the store and onto the sidewalk. Max waved at his friends, motioning them over.

The look on his face told them there wasn't going to be good news.

"Doc, you're up first," he said, somberly. "We got another body. Looks like the same cause of death as before. Only...this one is secured to the back wall."

Emil's face was somber as he entered the building. Torie gave Max an inquisitive look.

"Whoever did this, did a number on the place. I'm sorry. But also, you need to be prepared for something else," Max said.

Torie frowned, casting a look at Jasmin and Fionna. Together, the three of them entered the space they had been working so hard to create.

Torie gasped when she saw the extent of the damage inside the bakery. The long front counter meant to showcase the bakery products in a glass cabinet had been shattered. Their polished concrete countertops were smashed and broken, large chunks had been thrown about the space, some of them embedded in the very walls themselves.

Whoever, or whatever, had done this had been very strong.

There were only a couple of tables and chairs remaining. The ones that had been arranged along the far wall were broken and tossed about like a child's rag doll. The large fireplace which had been the center of the shop had been damaged as well. The flagstone facing had been broken and split in places. The stone mantle lay in pieces.

"What could have done this?" asked Jasmin.

"The same thing that probably did that." Fionna pointed to the wall behind the counter.

Their eyes followed her finger to a message written in red.

Give them back, or there will be more. There was an arrow pointing towards the swinging door behind the counter that led to the kitchen and supply area.

They walked slowly around the counter, pushing through the door to see Emil, back to them, examining the body of a woman.

Jasmin gasped and Fionna had to turn away briefly. Their response didn't go unnoticed by the medical examiner.

"Do you know this woman?" he asked.

Torie nodded. "Her name is Diedra Cain. She is…or was…our general contractor. She was working night and day to see that this place opened on time. She was probably here throughout the night because——" she paused, taking a deep breath, "——because I asked her to make sure the new wiring was ready for the oven upgrades that were being delivered."

Her voice was hard, yet still cracked as she spoke.

The woman's body was secured to the wall by two pieces of rebar driven through each of her shoulders. Her head slumped, but looking up into her face, they were able to see that her eyes were burned away, just like the body at the bus depot.

Emil turned to face them. "I'm sorry you have to see this. I'll have her taken down just as soon as I take a few more notes." He had his small, spiral notebook in his hand and had been scribbling furiously in it. There was a crunching of glass, and they turned just as Max and Terrance walked into the room. Max's face was dour, and Terrance had gone pale, his face clammy as he stared at the horror displayed before him.

"What kind of place is this? What is going on in this town?" he whispered.

Torie's eyes lit up as she faced him. "This is a town of good people. One that deserves better than this; and we're going to make sure whatever did this pays."

Her voice was like iron, and the young deputy could only nod in agreement.

"This is the work of a shifter," Max said. "The same one Elric and I fought, and you encountered at the Devil's Tramping Grounds."

"Are you sure?" asked Jasmin.

The werewolf nodded. "I'd recognize its stench anywhere."

"I'm finished with all my notes," said Emil. "We need to get her down and transferred to my office."

"I'll handle that," said Terrance. He took out his phone and hurried from the room.

"Poor guy. I don't think he has the stomach for this line of work," said Jasmin.

"No one should have the stomach for this," said Torie,

turning away. The tears that had been threatening to flow now rolled freely down her face.

The women made their way out of the defiled kitchen back to the counter space, where they stared at the writing on the wall. Jasmin waved a hand at the lettering, causing it to glow against the white backdrop of the wall.

"There is no residual magic underneath," she said. "Looks like this was just written in…blood. Probably by the shifter. I'm not getting any traces of magic, demonic or other, in the space. Fionna, are your senses picking up anything?"

The squirrel shifter shook her head. "Nothing. Just the scent of a shifter…bear. Mixed with something else…something I can't quite place." Her brow furrowed as she concentrated on dissecting everything she could from the area around her. Finally, she shook her head. "It may just be the residual scent of the workers that were in and out of the space."

Her eyes clouded as she looked at her friends. "Poor Diedra. She didn't deserve this."

"That monster is going to pay," said Torie. "Believe me."

"Did she have family in the area?" asked Jasmin.

Fionna shook her head. "No. This was her first job here. She moved up from Trinity Cove, trying to escape the horrors of that place. And look what happened to her…" She wiped at her tears. "Still, I'm going to make some calls; see if there is any next of kin somewhere we need to notify."

Jasmin nodded as Fionna turned to leave the building.

"This is my fault," said Torie. Her voice was soft and low, the words trembling from her mouth.

"No. It isn't. That demon is responsible for this. And together, we are going to make it pay," said Jasmin.

Torie didn't answer, her thoughts racing in her head. "How did it know where to find us?"

Jasmin shook her head. "I don't know. We fought it; so, I'm betting the bear tracked us here."

"It wants the girls back. If it could track us, why couldn't it track the women?"

Both witches looked at one another. Jasmin's jaw tightened as she scanned the room. "Maybe there is a reason for that."

She led them back into the kitchen where Max was standing. "Max, can you smell anything on this woman?"

The wolf looked puzzled, but then turned to face the body, his nostrils quivering slightly.

"Yes. I can smell everything on her, from the type of fabric softener she uses, where she was in town last night, down to the type of sweetener she puts in the coffee she drinks. Why?"

Suddenly, Torie understood what her friend was asking.

"Because when we found that body at the bus station, you couldn't pick up anything from it, remember? So, what makes this one different?" she asked.

"This isn't one of the disciples," said Max.

"Exactly. That means that the women are still safe for now. That's why the writing says to give them back. However, the shifter was able to track them earlier. What's preventing them from doing so now? Whatever the Fate sisters did, it must blind the women to senses, physical or magical," Torie added.

Jasmin was nodding. "Or maybe the wards around your house are blinding them. Otherwise, so much for the Fates not being able to use their powers in this world."

"Not necessarily," said Emil, turning to face them. "The Fates are indeed not of this realm. They come from the twilight space, an area between this world and many others. Kind of a nexus between multiple realities. Much like the demon Nerian, it could simply be that their particular magic is…acclimating to this realm. Perhaps when they arrived, they truly had no access to their powers. Much as the two of you would be limited in what you could do in the astral world."

Jasmin was nodding. "That makes sense. But why wouldn't they just tell us?"

"Would you tell someone on the astral plane that you just met, the extent of what you are capable of?" Emil asked.

"Good point. But they're the ones asking for help. The more we know the more help we can provide," Torie responded.

"There is something going on that we are missing," said Jasmin, raising a finger to tap at her lips. "I can feel it. They're not telling us something."

"Well, if that's the case, then you aren't asking the right questions," said Emil. "The Fates are forbidden from outright lying. They can evade and answer in a way that withholds information; but they can't lie to you."

"Well, that's good to know," said Torie. "Cos I still have questions."

Jasmin stared at her friend. "If you're talking about the remark they made about your heritage…don't go down that rabbit hole with them; they said it is not for them to reveal. You heard what Emil just said. They can lead you in almost any direction."

"He also said they can't lie," Torie replied.

"He is standing right here. And I would also add that,

for the record, I am aligned with Jasmin. The Fates are known to be fickle. Despite their dedication to maintaining the natural balance of things in this reality, they are also known for ultimately getting what they want," Emil stated. His stare intensified, his countenance stern. "And from where I sit, what they want is you."

Torie breathed deeply. She knew deep in the back of her mind that her friends were right. The sisters were hiding something. Her eyes brightened as she lit on an idea.

"You're right. They do want me. So why not use that to our advantage?"

Jasmin narrowed her eyes. "I don't think I like where this is going."

Torie wanted to offer her a smile of reassurance, but instead caught a glimpse of the innocent woman who had died in no small part because of her. She silently promised that no one else was going to die as long as she still drew breath. And if that meant taking herself out of the picture to prevent more harm, then so be it.

Chapter Eighteen

"Was it bad?" Shawn asked.

They were standing in the kitchen and Torie was sipping on a cup of tea, trying to steady her nerves. All she could do was nod, staring at her only child.

As usual, Leo had picked up on her mood and was pacing in circles on the kitchen island, his eyes never leaving Torie. His scales vibrated through the color spectrum as he tracked her every mood. Tiny wisps of steam escaped his nostrils from time to time as he scented at the air in her direction. Finally, wings vibrating, he lifted off the island to land on her shoulder, nuzzling against her face.

"He really loves you," Shawn said. "I can't believe the life you've made for yourself here. It's nothing short of amazing."

"Shawn, I know I haven't said this, but I'm really glad you're a part of this now. Keeping this part of myself from you was killing me. But I really thought I was doing the best thing for you; keeping you out of harm's way."

He smiled. "The old secret identity used by superheroes.

I get it. While you were out, I checked in on Elric and he told me some of the...adventures, you've had. Sounds like this town wouldn't still be here if it weren't for you."

Torie felt heat creeping across her cheeks at the compliment. It was truly such a relief to hear not only his acceptance, but also his praise of who and what she was. She knew how important it was for the child to be accepted for who they really were by the parent, but who knew the opposite was just as true?

Torie scratched at Leo's neck, tickling at the spot just below his snout that always made him vibrate with happiness. "Thank you as well for helping the disciples get settled in. I know this is probably a little——or a lot——overwhelming for you, but I promise we will get all of this sorted out."

Shawn held up a hand, letting her know thanks would not be necessary. "I will say, as big as this house is, it's officially full right now. I had to double up in the last bedroom, but they seemed fine with it."

"And the sisters? How have they been?"

Shawn exhaled sharply. "Honestly, I have no idea where they disappear to. One minute they're standing around talking to the disciples, the next, they just vanish. They may be in their room and just have the door shut; I can't tell." He hesitated, reaching up to give Leo a rub down his back. "Mom...do you trust them?"

"Of course she doesn't," came a voice from behind them.

They turned just as Corin walked into the kitchen, giving them both an ear-to-ear grin.

"Shawn, can you do me a favor? Go check on Elric for me. See if he needs anything."

Reluctantly, the young man agreed, leaving the kitchen

to his mother and the Fate. The two women locked eyes, neither wanting to be the first to break the stare.

Finally, Torie made her way to the sink. "Can I get you some tea, Corin?"

The elder woman smiled. "No, thank you, but I think I'll have some water if you don't mind." She headed toward the refrigerator, letting out a slight grunt as she pulled against the stainless-steel door.

"I want to trust you," said Torie. She faced Corin, her arms crossed as she leaned back, resting against the countertop behind her. "But I feel like you're not telling us everything."

Corin sipped her water and began fidgeting with the bottle cap, slipping it on and off as her eyes fixed on the witch.

"We have told you what you need to do in order to maintain balance," the Fate replied. "I don't know how more knowledge is going to help you. What else my sister and I may or may not see is immaterial at this point."

Torie was shaking her head. "No. You are asking me and my friends to risk our lives in order to save yours. And while it's nothing less than what we would do for anyone else, it's different if you have some hidden agenda we don't know about."

Corin raised her eyebrows. "I assure you we are not hiding anything. Yes, we have come to you for help, but I'm betting that even if we had not you still would be out there chasing down that demon, no matter if my sister and I were involved or not. It's what you do. You give of yourself without consideration of your own safety." She raised her hands looking around the room. "Look at this place you've built. It's not just for you. The fact that you've taken in so many strangers...that speaks to who you are, Torie. Maybe, what you should be asking yourself is why you feel the need to be a savior."

Torie blinked hard at the woman. "It's who I am. Maybe it's because I lived such a sheltered life, having someone I thought was taking care of me, only to find out they never really cared. Maybe I feel the need to show everyone that when I say I love you, it's not just lip service."

Her mouth snapped shut at that. She felt a stinging in her ears as her blood rushed to her head. Was it really as simple as that? She had never voiced it before, but nearly everything she felt she could trace back to her ex-husband and his betrayal. But why was that still bothering her? She had let it go long ago. The man had made his bed and was now lying in it. He was serving twenty-five years without parole for his part in a Ponzi scheme that had hurt so many people.

He had also taken the blame for Wednesday, his accomplice, mistress, and mother of his out-of-wedlock child. That added another fifteen years to his sentence. Fifteen years that he willingly accepted for the woman he loved.

And that was when it hit her.

Why had he been able to do that? He had a wife who had stood by his side since they were in college. One who had also bore him a son. Yet, he had spurned her and Shawn in favor of someone he had known a fraction of the amount of time. How had he fallen in love with someone else so quickly?

The answer had been simple; he never really loved Torie. Had he loved Shawn? That she didn't doubt; but when it came time to choose, she and their child had not made the cut.

Did all this mean that Torie was now overcompensating in some fashion? Was she willing to go so far above and beyond because she didn't want there to be any doubt in the minds of her new-found family that she meant what she said? Was it because she wanted to show them that anyone can profess love, but it's the actions behind the words that give it true meaning?

Corin was watching her with rapt attention. "Or could it be that you take on the role of protector because you're the only one with the kind of magic capable of dealing with all the horrors that come your way?"

Her words snatched Torie out of her reverie. "What? I'm so green to this whole witch thing that I'm sure I barely register on the supernatural front."

Corin wagged a finger. "Not true. Your hex gifts are very rare. The potential you have is unlike anything we Fates have seen in many generations." She watched as Torie considered her words. "Hex witches are very rare; but even among the elite, I sense that your magic is on a different level. I'm betting your friends know it as well. That's probably why they so desperately need you to remain among them."

"No. That's not true at all. I refuse to believe that."

Corin quickly offered a disarming smile, raising her hands in surrender to the witch. "I'm sorry. No offense intended. But I am betting your mother knew…"

That got Torie's attention and she squinted at the elderly woman. "Is that what you meant by the 'my heritage' remark from earlier?"

Corin just smiled. "In a way. But that isn't something we need to discuss. Not just yet at least." Torie opened her mouth to argue but Corin held up a stern finger. "Besides, you need to focus on more important tasks if you truly want to protect your friends and family. Namely, defeating that demon and his shifter accomplice. You know that every moment that passes, Nerian grows stronger. Soon, the demon may surpass you and your friends' abilities." She let that dangle in the air before giving it a sharp pull. "Your window to save your friends is closing."

"We are working on a plan," Torie offered. Though she couldn't quite dispel the tiniest bit of doubt in her words.

Corin nodded, heading out of the kitchen, before she turned back to face Torie once again.

"Oh, by the way, my sister and I couldn't help but notice the impressive amassment of magical tomes and artifacts in your study. Very impressive. Have you considered that there may be answers to what you need hidden within that fine collection?"

Torie frowned as the Fate walked away. Why had they been in her personal study? That area was part of her private wing and was generally off limits to any house guests. She would address that later, not only with the Fate sisters, but their disciples as well. Everything in that study had belonged to her mother and was irreplaceable. Still, it did give Torie pause.

What if Corin was right? Torie had yet to go through all of the books of spells and magical knick-knacks that had littered her mother's house. Maybe there was something there she and Jasmin could use. She placed Leo on the floor and took out some cubed pieces of steak for him. She smiled, watching as he ate greedily from his bowl, and then headed back to her study.

She strolled along the wall of books, trailing one hand gingerly along the leather spines. The back wall had larger shelves along it, on which a variety of objects were on display. The truth was, once she moved beyond the crystal ball and a twisted, highly polished stick which she assumed was a magic wand of some kind, she really didn't know what many of the objects did. They had been placed scattershot all over her mother's house, and when the elder hex witch had died, Torie had decided to gather them all in the study of her new home; imagining a time when she would be able to sit peacefully and learn about each object in kind.

Along with the collected mystical objects from her mother, the room also contained her own collection of pieces she had acquired during her time in Singing Falls. There were the fangs of a vampire who had once tried to kill her, various casks containing the sacred organs of shifters, a bit of magical clay once used to animate a golem, and a dagger that a hunter had tried to stab her with.

That last one she had offered to Jasmin. The hunter in question had been her daughter; but her best friend had wanted nothing to do with it. Torie stared at the black dagger and tried to imagine Shawn wielding it while trying to kill her. Yeah, no wonder Jasmin felt the way she did.

She made a mental note to give the blade to Max so that he could see it properly destroyed, and then turned her attention to myriad books and scrolls that made up the main shelf. How was she ever going to find what she needed in those missives?

Once, not long ago, she had used a spell that allowed what she sought to reveal itself to her, separating itself from the rest of the books.

But this was different. She didn't know what she was truly up against, so how would she know what spell to call for?

"Why am I just now thinking about sorting through this? I really should have memorized everything my mother had to offer."

And just like that, she felt a light bulb click on in her mind. Could she do it? Was it even possible?

She reached for her phone to call Jasmin, but then thought better of it. She would just lecture Torie, telling her that what she was thinking was dangerous and untried.

Torie put her phone down on the desk in front of the shelves and stared at the books.

It might be untried, but…that didn't mean it couldn't be done. She moved to the center of the room and closed her eyes. She held her arms out to either side and cleared her mind, taking a couple of deep breaths before she began to chant.

"I open my heart, I open my mind,
let all things flow through space and time.
I summon to me all that now stands tethered,
to enter my being, no longer bound by leather."

The air slowly began to shimmer around the witch. Slowly, the books on the shelf began to glow in a warm yellow light. A light that expanded, pulsing in a low cadence until it shot forward with blinding speed, striking Torie and engulfing her in a blinding nimbus.

She screamed and her body stiffened as her brain felt like someone had stabbed it with a red-hot poker. Her eyes flew open briefly before fluttering closed as she fell, the floor rushing up to meet her as she lost consciousness.

Chapter Nineteen

The feel of wet silk gliding along her face was the first thing Torie felt as she made her way out of the darkness that engulfed her. She raised a hand, clumsily pushing the silk cloth away, only to realize it wasn't a piece of cloth.

It was a tongue.

Attached to a very concerned little dragon. Torie attempted to push Leo off her and sit up, but a familiar voice drifted to her ears.

"Hey, take it easy there. We need to make sure you didn't hit your head." It was Elric, sitting beside her, softly stroking her hand. "I tried to keep the little fella off you, but that was impossible."

Torie looked around, taking in the shapes around her.

"What happened?" she asked.

"We were hoping you could tell us." It was Shawn, who was kneeling to her other side, one hand on her shoulder.

"How is she?" asked Jasmin from the doorway, her cell to her ear. "I've got Emil on the phone; he can be here in a just a bit. Glen is also on her way over."

Torie sat up, rolling her eyes slightly. "No…I'm fine. None of that. Please thank Emil for the offer, but I'm not dead. There isn't anything he can do for me." She returned the stare Jasmin was giving her. "Honestly, I'm okay. Other than feeling a little stupid at causing all this commotion."

She was happy to see Jasmin nod, then step out of the room, whispering to Emil. Turning her attention to Elric, she placed a hand on the side of his face.

"Elric, what are you doing down here? You should still be in bed. How are you feeling?"

The werewolf smiled down at her. "I'm a wolf. We heal fast, remember?"

She struggled for a moment to sit completely upright, waving her hand at any protests, and then slowly got to her feet. Making her way to the closest chair, she plopped down.

"Here, drink this," said Jasmin, returning to the room with a glass of cold water.

The liquid felt good going down, easing a slightly bitter taste sitting in the back of Torie's throat. Just then, Fionna and Glen burst into the space, rushing to their friend's side.

Torie smiled warmly, attempting to reassure them everything was fine. "You didn't have to come. I am perfectly fine."

Glen was on one knee in front of her, placing a blood pressure cuff around one arm. "And that's good to know. That doesn't mean I can't check your blood pressure and listen to your heart and lungs. Now sit back and relax."

Torie did as she was instructed, looking around the room at her friends and family as they waited anxiously for Glen to finish her assessment.

"All her vitals appear to be in the normal range," said Glen, returning her equipment to her bag. "Whatever happened seems to have passed."

"Mom, what *did* happen?" asked Shawn, stooping down in front of her, one hand resting on his mother's knee.

She swallowed the dryness in her throat, looking sheepishly about the room. "Well, I tried a spell…and it seems to have maybe gone a little awry. That's all. These things happen." She hoped she sounded more convincing than she felt.

Jasmin crossed her arms, giving her a hard stare. "Oh, really? Because whatever you did rang out like a magical Liberty Bell. It freaked out Leo, and I felt it at my house. Came running to make sure you were okay."

Torie swallowed hard, unable to keep her friend's gaze. "I didn't mean to scare anyone. But I was looking for something…anything that could give us an advantage in our fight with this demon."

"Well, as long as you're okay, I'm all for you doing what you have to in order to find this monster and stop it." It was Fionna who spoke up, her voice hardening. "That poor woman did not deserve to die that way. She was kind and helpful and just wanted to do the job she loved doing. And to be killed like that…no. This Nerian has to pay, and I hope you found a way to do it."

Torie took a deep breath. Leave it to Fionna to break everything she felt down into succinct words. The only thing her friend had left out was the fact that Torie was to blame. She grimaced slightly as she leaned forward to set her water down. She was pleasantly surprised that the coaster at the far side of the coffee table slid across to land perfectly under the glass before it could contact the wood.

Elric arched an eyebrow. "You know, seeing that reminds me. While I was kind of in and out upstairs, I remember things like this happening. The blankets covering me when I was chilled, the bathroom door opening and closing when I approached it…what is going on here?"

Torie raised her shoulders, looking up at her boyfriend. "I don't——" But she stopped. Looking around the room, eyes wide, her mouth dropped in surprise.

"Torie? What is it? What's wrong?" asked Jasmin, alarmed.

"Oh my God. Is she having a stroke?" demanded Shawn, his hands flying up to cover his mouth.

"No. No, baby, I'm fine," said Torie. Her voice was soft and trembled slightly as she looked around the room. "It's just that…everything is so…beautiful. I can't describe it."

Everyone looked around, trying to see whatever it was that now captivated Torie. She was standing, her eyes flitting back and forth at things around her. She held one hand in the air, palm up, moving it slowly to and fro, almost as if she were trying to entice a butterfly or a hummingbird to land there.

"I see so much," she whispered. She turned to face her friends and froze, staring in disbelief. "Incredible…you're all so exquisite."

They were glowing; or more precisely, they were suffused with a different color and depth of light that swirled and moved within them. She laughed. Her friends looked like human lava lamps.

"I can't believe what I'm seeing. Everywhere I look there are threads of light and floating sigils. And you, all of you… have your own light and look. Elric, you and Fionna are dark purple, with pulses of black coming from inside you." She turned, looking at Glen. "Glen, you look the same, but you have a white aura surrounding you. I don't know how I know this, but your look is that of a normal human. Jasmin, oh my, you're orange! Bright and sparkly, just like the sigils and the threads running through the air around me." She looked down at her own hands. "We are the same color, you and I."

"What about me, Mom?"

She spun to stare at her son. And her face dropped.

"Shawn, you're human as well." Her mouth widened, drawing up into a smile at her son. "So pure and beautiful."

She felt a vibration pass through the air; unlike any she had ever felt. Almost as if someone had struck a giant tuning fork onto her. She glanced down, instinctively realizing it was coming from Leo. The little dragon sat at her feet, and she was immediately lost in the brilliance he cast off. Like his own scales, his form ran a gamut of colors, shimmering through the spectrum in random waves.

Again, she felt the vibrations he gave off and she held out her hand, feeling them bounce off her.

Magic. Leo radiated pure magical energy; much like what she was feeling coming from the house. But how was that possible? The home was brand new construction, built to her standards. Granted, it was built across ley lines, but going by what Jasmin had told her, it took decades, sometimes centuries, for ambient magical energy from inside the earth to leech into a home.

They also hadn't performed any large spells or incantations—— She stopped in her tracks, thoughts frozen.

"Jasmin, the spell we performed to empower the kitchen...could it have taken on a life of its own? Could that be why the spell we thought contained to the kitchen is now acting out in other areas of the house?"

Jasmin looked perplexed as she considered the question. "I don't understand. Why would you ask that?"

"Because I can see magic flowing through the house. I can see all kinds of things...like the fact that shifters are made up of one type of magic, you and I are a different kind, and Glen appears as a normal human. Well, Glen and Shawn, I mean. But the magical signatures flowing throughout the house, matches what you and I have. When we automated the cleaning process in the kitchen, I think the spell somehow spread. Despite the fact we contained it." She thought of her mom briefly, and a bit of sadness flickered over her face. "That would explain all the weird going's on around here. The house is doing what my subconscious is asking for."

Jasmin frowned, chewing lightly at her thumbnail. "I suppose that could be possible. But I'm more concerned that you're seeing magic, and auras and whatever else. What kind of spell did you cast?"

"Well, I thought it was a shortcut spell. I thought maybe there could be something in my mom's grimoires that could help us in our fight with this demon thing, so I cast a spell to help me absorb the knowledge from the books quickly... rather than hunt through them and try to find what we need." She looked about again, once more distracted by the threads of magic in the air.

"That was a dangerous spell, Torie. Who knows what ramifications it could have," Jasmin replied.

"Could it hurt her?" Elric asked, moving to stand next to Torie.

"Of course not," came a voice from just outside the room.

They turned just as Vera and Corin stepped into the space.

"It isn't the knowledge we possess that is dangerous, but rather what we choose to do with it," continued Corin.

Everyone turned towards the two sisters, including

Torie. The witch stared at them, or rather, she stared in their general direction.

"Tell me, Torie, how do we look to your newborn eyes?" asked Vera.

Torie blinked rapidly, then pinched the bridge of her nose between her thumb and forefinger, squeezing her eyes tightly shut before opening them again.

"I...I don't see anything. You're not there," she managed. "I can make out a vague, outline that seems to be flickering in and out. But for the most part, nothing."

"Interesting," said Corin, looking at her sister. "In all honesty, you shouldn't be able to see anything at all where we are concerned."

Some of the disciples had started to congregate in the hall just outside the study, and Torie stared at the few that stuck their heads in the doorway, curious as to what all the commotion was about.

"Is everything okay?" one of them asked. "We heard loud voices. Are we in trouble? Is it the bear again?" Her voice trembled and shot up a couple of octaves.

"No. Everything is fine," said Vera. "Take your sisters and return to your rooms. We'll be up soon for your guided meditations."

After they disappeared, the attention turned back to Torie. She shook her head slowly, taking a few deep breaths.

"It's clearing," she said. "Everything is returning to normal." She wasn't sure if she was happy or sad that she was no longer seeing magic all around her.

"I think you need to go lie down," said Elric.

She waved him off. "There isn't time. I think I know how to deal with that demon. But first things first. We must stop that bear shifter, and I'm pretty sure I know how to find him as well."

"Fine. But I want you to at least eat something and rest a bit before making any more decisions," said Elric.

Torie smiled and nodded. Everyone filed out of the office, heading toward the main wing of the house. Jasmin and Torie were the last ones to leave the room and Torie grabbed at her arm, bidding her to hang back for just a minute.

"Hey, what is it? Are you really okay?" Jasmin asked.

Torie nodded. "I am. A bit of a headache, but that's to be expected. I absorbed so much of the knowledge my mother had written down over her lifetime. I have so much to share with you. But first...I'm scared, Jasmin."

Her friend turned, grasping her by the arms. "What is it? I know you saw something you aren't telling us. What was it?"

Torie swallowed briefly. "It was the Fates. The fact that they are like a...void...of magic. There is literally nothing there."

"Well, they did say they are from an in between, an area that their kind live in, that our magic can't touch. That could explain why you can't see them."

Torie was nodding. "Yes, I thought of that. But the thing is...when I first looked at Shawn, he appeared the same way to me. He wasn't there; just a vague outline of his body, and then he kind of shimmered into focus."

Jasmin didn't say anything as she stared at her friend.

"Jasmin. I'm afraid that my son is something other than a witch. And it terrifies me."

Chapter Twenty

"Do you know how ridiculous I feel?" Torie was sitting in her bed, back propped up against pillows, as Elric covered her with a large, downy blanket. He had placed a collection of magazines and the television remote next to her. Leo was curled up on a pillow beside her, eyes closed as he snored gently.

Elric glared at her, but only in the most loving kind of way.

"I told you I'm fine," she continued. "Even Glen said my headache is nothing more than a reflection of the sudden change in my blood pressure that made me pass out in the first place."

"With all due respect to Glen, I will feel better if you take it easy for a bit. She will be back to check on you later this evening so until then, you are to stay put and rest," he said.

Torie sighed. "Jasmin, help me out here. You know I'm fine." She looked over at her best friend standing in the doorway holding a wooden tray with a cup of tea and a bowl of soup atop it.

Jasmin opened her mouth to respond but caught the hardened look Elric shot her.

"You know what? I'm staying out of this one. It might not be the worst thing in the world for you to rest up a bit," Jasmin answered.

"Do you think the demon is resting up?" Torie seethed, a bitterness undercutting her tone that she hadn't intended on letting slip out. She took a deep breath, releasing the edge that had crept into her voice. "I'm sorry. I just feel like I need to be out there doing something."

Elric stared at her. "There is a lot of 'I' in that sentence. This isn't just on you, Torie." His tone was almost hurtful as he looked away.

"I think I'm going to just sit this here and go check on Fionna," said Jasmin. She sat the tray gently on the bed, and backed out of the room, closing the door silently after her.

Neither of them spoke, each regarding the person they cared most about in the world.

"Elric, I'm sorry. I didn't mean to imply that your help isn't welcome. It's just that you're hurt, and I can't risk another person's——"

He cut her off mid-sentence with a slight huff. "Why are you apologizing for your thoughts, Torie? I know you well enough to know that, even if you mean it, it won't change your behavior when it comes to things like this."

She was stung by his words. More-so by the fact that she recognized the truth in them more than anything else. It wasn't like she hadn't heard it before.

"I know. You're right. And this is something I absolutely

am working on. And I intend to keep working on it, but right now——"

"There is always going to be a 'right now', Torie. There is always going to be something looming that will threaten to kill us or wipe out the town, or who knows what. You ever stop to think that all these people you so willingly risk your life for, would do the same for you if given the chance? You're not alone here; unless you want to be."

He turned to walk out of the room, pausing just as he got to the door. Torie wasn't sure if he had more to say or he was waiting for her to reply. Neither spoke, and he left the room quietly; the only sound the low-pitched rumbling of Leo as he snored contentedly next to her.

She knew that Elric's words were coming from a place of love; and she also knew that if things were reversed, she would be behaving the same way. She picked up the soup, taking a sip from the spoon. Potato, leek, and bacon. She closed her eyes, enjoying the creamy warmth while making a mental note to get the recipe from Jasmin so they could add this to the menu at the bakery.

Thinking about their business helped to steady her thoughts, giving her something to focus on. But that led to her mind replaying the devastating discovery of the body and the senseless destruction of their property.

Couldn't Elric see that she was fighting to make Singing Falls safe for everyone? And it could never really be that if every demon and monster strolling through felt like they could make this town its own personal food bank.

No. She wasn't going to allow this to continue. Fionna had been so distraught at what happened. She knew the squirrel shifter understood her.

She sat her bowl down as an idea came to her. She

closed her eyes, steadied her breathing, and focused on a single thought.

Fionna.

The shifter should still be in the house, but there was no trace of her.

She let her mind drift, floating through in search of her friend. It was something she had been able to do previously with Elric, but she had never attempted it with another. New magic focused her will as she tracked her friend through the woods and across town in the span of a few heartbeats. One of the first magical gifts to reveal itself to her after turning forty was the ability to understand and speak with shifters in their animal forms.

But more likely than not, Fionna would be in human form now. Torie wasn't sure if she would be able to make contact, but she felt her power singing within her as the scenery flew past her mind's eye. The trees blurred, and she knew what it was like to experience the freedom of a bird; careless and free as it drifted along held aloft by the caressing winds.

Was it her imagination, or could she actually feel the gentle brush of the air passing across her skin? The soft tickle as it played through her hair as she sailed onward.

The feeling was captivating. Intoxicating.

How simple it might be to stay here, continuing to soar along, leaving the cares of everything that pulled at her behind. What if she angled her consciousness straight up? Would she eventually enter the blackness of space? And what lay beyond that? Could she just keep floating upward, away from——

No. She felt her body tense in rejection of what had tried to creep unbidden into her mind. Where had that even come from? She didn't have time to ponder the question as she felt a pull in the back of her mind. She focused and then noticed a tiny, glowing bit of purple that stood out in the mass of gray rushing past.

Fionna.

No sooner had she thought her friend's name than she was suddenly "standing" in front of the shifter. Torie smiled. She should have known Fionna would be at the bakery. She was surrounded by cleaning supplies and was working to restore order to the vandalized space. She had a large sponge in her gloved hand and was staring at the dried blood on the wall where their contractor had been killed.

"Fionna," Torie said. It felt weird trying to use her physical voice in what was most definitely not her physical body.

The squirrel shifter jumped, dropping her sponge as she spun around. Red, watery eyes grew large as she stared in Torie's direction.

"Torie? Is that you? How...and what, are you doing here?"

"It is. In the...not-so-flesh, I suppose. Can you see me?"

Fionna winced, placing a hand to her ear. "I can. You look, I don't know, like you, just more glittery and see-through. Like a bedazzled ghost. But I can definitely hear you. Maybe don't scream at me?"

Torie frowned. "I'm not screaming. But are you *hearing* me in your ears or in your head?"

Fionna frowned, her eyes narrowing in concentration. "Now that you mention it, I do hear you in my head."

Torie nodded. "I'm not exactly sure how this works. But I think you should get used to my voice soon enough." She took a close look at her friend. "Were you crying?"

Fionna wiped at her face. "I just wanted to clean this place up a bit. Terrance came by and said it was okay to clean. They have all the evidence they need for the investigation, and I just want to get an idea for when we can plan the opening." She looked away, unable to meet her friend's ghostly gaze.

"That isn't true, is it?" asked Torie. She was hoping her mental voice was able to convey the empathy she was feeling.

Fionna looked down at her feet. "No. I feel so bad for what happened. This place was my idea; I feel like I forced you all into it. And now look. Because of that, an innocent woman is dead."

Again, tears wracked her frame, and she threw her arms around herself. "For once, I just want to do something meaningful for this town and not have it end in blood and death. I just want to make a real difference."

Torie wished she had arms to hold and comfort her friend with. All she could do was sympathize and hope the shifter would agree with her plan.

"Fionna, that's why I'm here. I need your help with something."

Fionna looked up, her tears slowing. "Anything."

Torie told her what she had planned, and the shifter's eyes grew wide.

"Are you sure that will work?" Fionna asked.

"No. But it's all I can think of at the moment."

Fionna nodded as she chewed on her bottom lip. "Does Jasmin know? And what did Elric think about this?"

Her hesitation told Fionna everything; even before words were spoken. "Jasmin went to find you, so she is probably still back at my house. Neither of them know I'm here. My body is home, confined to bed rest. Rest I don't need." She saw the look of concern on her friend's face and continued. "As I said to them, I'm fine. And like you, I don't want to ever see something like this happen again. I just need you to help me find him. That's all."

Fionna heaved a sigh as she stared at her friend. "I'm in. I'll do what I can. But why can't you just locate him the same way you did me? And then float on over to him."

"It's not the same. I was able to find you because I *know* you. I know how you feel when I'm close to you. I don't know this one, however. But I figure that with your shifter senses, you can get us close enough, then my new mystical vision can point him out to me. That's the hope at least."

She didn't sound very convincing. Hope wasn't a strategy after all, but it was all she had at the moment.

"Okay, are you ready for this part?" Torie asked.

Fionna exhaled sharply and shrugged. "Ready as I'll ever be."

"Alright. Just relax, and don't fight it."

Torie whispered a silent incantation and glided forward until her non-corporeal self entered that of her friend. She could feel the magic working through them both as she settled into Fiona's mind as a hitchhiker.

In a flash, Fionna shifted into her squirrel form and scattered out of the bakery, around the shop and headed for the woods.

"Okay then," said Torie. "Let's go find us a bear shifter."

Chapter Twenty-One

She had thought the experience would be akin to the sense of flying when she had first sought out Fionna. But it was nothing like that. In flight, she was alone, removed from any connection to physical sensation. But here, running through the forest and trees accompanying the squirrel shifter, the intimate touch of the ground and forest was everywhere.

Dry leaves crunched beneath her feet, bits of grit and sand felt like walking across beads cloaked in the finest of silks. The smell of tree bark, grass and clover regaled her senses as they sped along in leaps and bounds. And everywhere around there was sound; unlike anything she had experienced before.

She had done something similar with Elric once, viewing the world through his eyes, but it had not come close to the complete immersion she felt with Fionna.

"Are you sure you have its scent?" Torie asked.

"Yes," came Fiona's mental reply. Now that she was in her animal form, the connection between them was crystal clear. "That monster's scent was everywhere in the bakery.

It was all I could do not to go after it myself, so I'm actually glad you suggested this."

Unlike her previous mind meld with Elric, Torie retained control of her senses independently from Fionna. As the squirrel sped along, Torie was able to raise her awareness, looking around them. She recognized this part of the forest. They were headed towards the base of the large waterfall the town was named for.

She listened closely to the bell-like sounds of the water breaking across rocks and bits of crystalline structures as it tumbled down the face of the mountain. She had never heard their beauty through the ear of a shifter and her heart swelled at the beautiful sounds of the tumbling waters.

Fionna stopped moving and Torie felt a chill race up her spine. They listened, ears perked to hear the slight, soft crunch being masked by the waterfall. The scent of moss, wet wood and dirt gave way to the reek of dried blood and rancid breath.

Together, they turned, scanning the large riverbed the falls emptied into. And there, on the opposite side of the lake, a figure emerged. A man, large in stature, stood rocking back and forth, moving his massive weight from one foot to the other as he coldly regarded them. Torie stared, focusing her vision on the man. He was composed of swirling purple light, the color of shifters. But there was something wrong with his light. Darkness gathered in the center of him, pulsing in a manner that dispersed the purple.

The bear shifter.

Fionna could hear the man growl, deep and rumbling, it came from his chest, echoing across the river. They watched as he slowly walked to where the river narrowed and sloshed his way through the shallow water towards them.

"What do we do?" asked Fionna. "Can you zap him or something?"

Torie froze. She hadn't considered the need to use magic. Would she be able to utilize her spells in this form?

"Fionna, we just needed to find out where he's staying. Can you tell if his scent is stronger around here?"

The squirrel shifter was nodding. "Oh, it's all over the place. This is definitely where he's been holed up." She began to slowly back away from the advancing shifter. "Maybe we should run."

"No. That's not what we came here for. If the demon is using this creature as his eyes, ears and fists...then maybe it's time we level the playing field by taking him out."

"Um, isn't this the same shifter that took on both Max and Elric and nearly killed them?"

Torie could hear the nervousness in her friend's voice. But rather than focus on that, she concentrated on what she didn't hear.

Fear.

There was no fear in Fionna; her heartbeat was strong and steady, despite the tremor Torie sensed in her words. And that was when Torie realized she wasn't afraid for herself, but rather, what would happen if she were slain in this form. Would it also mean Torie's death as well?

Torie could see the thought in Fionna's mind and tried her best to banish it from the shifter's head. It turned out neither of them had time to dwell on the subject as the man suddenly leapt at them, shifting to a bear in midair as he came down with a thud that shook the ground and charged them. From her perspective, Torie had never seen an animal so large; one of its claws was larger than Fionna's entire body.

Without thinking, Torie whispered an incantation,

throwing out magic to the earth beneath the great bear. Dirt and rock softened, turning to muck, sucking the bear into its belly. The shifter roared, trying to rear up on its hind legs, but couldn't as Torie reversed her spell, returning the ground to its more solid density.

The bear was stuck, held fast in the hardened earth, and it roared its defiance as Fionna approached. Then, it settled down, glaring at the little squirrel, each exhale of its breath was a blast furnace, ruffling her fur.

Torie projected her thoughts at the beast. "I know what you're thinking. Go ahead, shift back into your human form. Your bear form is barely capable of surviving the pressure being applied to hold you locked in place. Do you really think you'll fare better as a man?"

The bear glared at them through yellow eyes, not moving. Torie couldn't be sure, but was…he smiling at them? Why on Earth would——

Fionna sensed the attack a heartbeat before Torie did and leapt to the side, sprinting away just as a blast of heat scorched the ground where she had been standing. She wheeled around, scouring the area behind them. Torie instinctively threw up a protective barrier as they stared at an unassuming young man who had somehow managed to get the drop on them, evading both Fionna's senses and Torie's mystical perceptions.

He was dressed in jeans with a pressed, long-sleeved white button-up shirt. He smiled at them, showing dazzling white teeth, and gave them a nod. Neatly trimmed blond hair capped a handsome, narrow face. He waved, his hand still glowing from the blast of fire that had nearly incinerated Torie and Fionna.

"Hi there," he said. His voice was melodious and friendly. "I don't know who you are, little squirrel, but I do believe that's none other than Torie Bliss hitching a ride with you. Cute trick." He took one slow step towards them, his smile disappearing. "Do you know who I am?"

Torie projected her thoughts loudly at the man. "Nerian."

His smile returned. "That's one name, certainly. Of course, no one other than those three old bags, the Fates, call me that." He held out his arms and did a quick spin around. "Do you like this form? Is it less threatening to you? I borrowed it from someone I used to know."

Torie could feel the tension in Fionna's body as the squirrel shifter's flight or fight response began to spool up. She reached out with her mind, trying to calm her.

"Are you going to free my friend there?" asked the demon, nodding in the trapped bear's direction.

"No. I don't think so. Not just yet," said Torie.

The demon cocked his head to one side. "You don't need him anymore. I mean, you came here to kill him, right? But only after he told you where to find me. Well, I'm right here, so you don't need him anymore."

Fionna was backing slowly away as the demon inched closer to them.

He stopped when he saw how skittish she was becoming. "Don't worry. Unlike you, I don't have murder on my mind." He smiled, pursing his lips. "Not yet at least."

"If that's meant to scare us, it doesn't," said Torie. "I hear you're not up to your full potential just yet."

Nerian laughed, taking them in. "Trust me. I don't need to be at full strength to take out a witch and her...tiny shifter friend. If I wanted to, you would both be dead already."

Torie stirred, keeping her focus on the barrier around them. "Yeah? So why haven't you?"

"Because I have no interest in killing you. I need something from you."

Torie swallowed hard. "Yeah. We got your message. You want to know where the disciples are? You're not getting anywhere near them."

The demon threw his head back as laughter erupted from him. "Is that what you were told?" He raised both hands and slowly took two steps back from them. "Why would I want a couple of human children? What possible good could they do me?"

"The Fates said you were after them," Torie replied.

Nerian shook his head. "The Fates are using those women as a smoke screen. They imbue them with just enough of their essence to throw me...and my associates... off their trail. We can't 'see' them so to speak, as long as they are surrounded by their disciples. The Fates use those women to mask their presence in this world. That's why they gather them around."

"Back at the Black Pit...or Devil's Tramping Ground, why was the bear trying to kill them if they aren't a threat to you?"

"I assure you he was not trying to kill them. He was simply gathering them all in one place. Once they were inside that pit, the cloak they give off would have been contained and the Fates would have been revealed to me. I was so close...until you and your friend came along."

Torie frowned. "So, the message to give them back...?"

"Was meant for the Fates," Nerian said.

"What do you want with them?" Torie asked.

He smiled again, flashing those pearly whites. "Well, the reason they gave you is probably true. I need to finish what was started with them."

Torie felt Fionna bristle. Again, she reached out to calm the shifter. "They said you killed their sister."

"I assure you I did not. I am merely taking advantage of the opportunity that death has caused. They are keeping a gate closed that I want open. And the only way to open it is to kill all three of them. And the window to do that is narrowing. I need to do it before they find a replacement for their slain sister." He stared at her, his eyes narrowing. "I'm pretty sure they have found who they want to replace her; they just need their new sister to accept the role." His smile faded and he licked his lips. "There is no coven in Singing Falls for them to select from. There is only you and your friend. So that means in order for me to succeed, either you or the other witch must fall."

Torie felt anger rising inside her, causing her voice to tremble slightly. "And you honestly think I'm going to just stand around and let you do that?"

The demon shrugged. "I don't care what you do. You really aren't that much of a concern for me. But I will make you a deal. I've been told that you have something in your possession I need. Give it to me, along with the two Fates, and I will let you and the other witch live. Give them to me and I promise you will never see me again." His words did little to convey any sense of trust to the witch. "Why are you protecting them? If the roles were reversed, rest assured they would not hesitate to hand you over."

Despite herself, Torie felt a bit of intrigue. "Other than the Fates, what is it you think I have?"

"A key. One that will allow me to permanently split the veil that separates your world from mine. After the Fates are dead, of course."

"I don't have anything like that. So, you're out of luck."

The demon stared hard at her, then held out his hand.

Black smoke appeared and slowly morphed into an image above his open palm. "Do you recognize this?"

Torie stared. It was the black knife she held in her study. The one Jasmin's hunter-daughter had tried to kill them with.

"No," she said. But she knew it was too late. She felt the chilling touch of something crawling through her mind in a flash. It was quick, like the feel of walking along peacefully and suddenly stepping into an unseen spider web.

"Aw…there it is," said the demon, his eyes taking on an eerie blackness.

Torie didn't move. Instead, she focused her magic, calling it up within her. She consciously slipped free of Fionna's mind and body. She emerged, ethereal and glowing with power from the squirrel shifter, as she stepped free.

The demon stared at her, that annoying grin still plastered across his face. "You realize that in this form, you are literally a shade of your true self. You are no real threat to me."

He stared at the bear shifter to his right and, raising a fist, threw a bolt of fire into the ground, shattering the earth and freeing the creature.

"And you certainly aren't a match for both of us."

Torie smiled in return. "You have no idea who you're dealing with, demon."

Magic flared to life around her as she held out one hand towards the demon and the other towards the bear.

"Besides, I just have to keep you busy for a bit."

The demon looked around. "Where is the tiny shifter?" He turned to the bear and motioned with his hand. Immediately, the creature lurched into the woods, nose down as it ran. "Sending her for reinforcements won't work. They won't be coming."

Torie smiled, drawing on more magic as she made ready to attack. "You underestimate my friends."

The demon laughed. "And you underestimate me. Do you really think you're the only person who can be in two places at once?"

Torie felt something claw at her heart, and her eyes grew wide. She reached for the tether that connected her to the space her consciousness was occupying and severed it.

In a flash of light and imagery, she felt herself boomerang back into her physical body. She opened her eyes and senses to the sound of chaos all around.

Chapter Twenty-Two

Fighting off the nausea that accompanied the sudden return to her body, Torie made her way to her feet, throwing off the blanket that covered her.

"Elric! Shawn!" she called, holding onto the wall for balance as she made her way out of the bedroom. She stumbled, unsure of her balance, down the long hallway towards the back stairs leading to the kitchen. At the top of the stairs a flicker of light caught her attention. As she got closer, she saw a wall of green flames shooting up from the stairwell.

Immediately, she threw an arm across her face to protect herself from the fire, but quickly realized the flames, despite their intensity, were actually burning *cold*.

Leo.

She called the dragon's name, shouting to be heard above the sounds of shouting and screaming coming from the lower level of the house.

"Leo!" she tried again, this time adding a mental push to the dragon as well.

The flames died down at once and she saw the dragon sitting midway down the staircase. Black smoke curled from his nostrils as he took flight and made his way to her shoulder. He was vibrating so hard that it was almost painful to her, but still she did her best to calm him.

With the last of the dragon fire dying down, she made her way down the steps where the first of the disciples lay. Torie reached out with her magic as she neared the woman. The girl was alive, though unconscious, a large abrasion across her forehead.

As she made her way through the kitchen, there were signs of chaos everywhere. Broken cabinets, a multitude of broken dishes and glasses, and everywhere she looked there were signs of a fracas.

There were more sounds of a struggle, followed by breaking glass, coming from the back of the house.

Her study.

She rushed down the back hall, stepping over more of the disciples that her magic told her were still alive, but unconscious.

"Shawn!" she screamed again.

"…Torie…in here," came a voice.

It was from the study, and she rushed in to find Jasmin trying to get to her feet. The witch grasped her side, her breath catching as she grimaced. Her lower lip was bleeding, but other than that, she seemed to be alright.

Torie bent down. "Jasmin! What happened? Where are Elric and Shawn?"

Jasmin was holding her head, trying to steady herself in her friend's grasp. "Elric…went to help Max. Shawn…oh no…he took Shawn."

Torie felt her blood run cold. "Who? Who took my son?"

"It was Terrance…that leopard shifter that works with Max."

Torie was stunned as she helped her friend to the couch to sit down. "Tell me what happened."

"We were all in the kitchen; Elric, me, a couple of the disciples, when there was a knock at the door. It was Terrance. He said Max had a lead on the bear that attacked them and it was over on the east ridge…that there were reports of another girl being attacked up there. He said Max wanted Elric to meet him up there, because he knows the terrain better than anyone else in the police department. He said Max told him to watch over us here at the house. Something felt off about the whole thing, but it all happened so fast."

"Why didn't you wake me?"

She shook her head. "Elric said you needed the rest. He said he and Max would handle it. As soon as he left, the shifter attacked us. He hit me with something. Something that was magic in nature. It…stunned me, wrapped me in a spell of some kind that I've never felt before; and then he attacked the women." She coughed, wincing at the effect it had on her body. "I couldn't focus my magic, but Leo appeared and I…I told him not to let anyone up the stairs, to protect you. Then, I could hear Shawn calling for you…"

Tears flowed from Torie's eyes. Her hand trembled as it covered her mouth.

"I tried to stop him, but my head was ringing. They were in the back hall, just outside your office. Shawn tried to use his power, but the leopard was just too much. He subdued him in no time…and that was it. He took off with him. Out the back, over the fence and out of sight before I could react."

Torie felt as if someone had just punched her in the

stomach, knocking the wind from her lungs. She plopped down on the couch, her mind reeling.

Her son. The light of her life. In the hands of that demon.

Her eyes narrowed at the thought of that monster and his big smile and loud laughs. He had been playing her. Toying with her and Fionna in order to buy time for his minion to do this.

She looked up, rushing to her bookshelf where she saw the black dagger still sitting where she had left it. Why hadn't he taken it when he had the chance?

Her thoughts were interrupted by the sound of feet rushing down the hall towards them. Instantly, Torie was standing, her hands glowing as she turned to face the opening to the study. Despite her pain, Jasmin was also on her feet, a ball of orange magic summoned and at the ready.

Fionna didn't realize just how close she came to being obliterated by the two witches as she hurtled through the doorway.

Torie breathed a sigh of relief as she dropped her magic. "Fionna! Are you okay? Where is the bear shifter?"

Fionna was breathing hard and bent over slightly to catch her breath. "I've no idea. He was chasing me through the woods, and then suddenly he just stopped, turned and veered off. I headed back here as quickly as I could." She stood, still breathing heavily as she looked at Torie. "I tried to lead him back here. What happened with the demon? And I'm glad to see you back to being flesh and blood again."

Jasmin stared in response. "Torie, what is she talking about?"

Torie stammered, shaking her head. "I'll explain later.

Right now, I need to find Shawn." She looked around the room. "Where are the Fate sisters?"

Jasmin shook her head. "There was no sign of them during the attack. They seem to have a habit of disappearing when needed."

Torie was nodding. "Yeah, well enough is enough. It's their disciples in danger, and as a result, so too is my son. And they aren't lifting a finger to help us. Well, no more." She narrowed her eyes, focusing on her newly acquired mystical vision before locking onto something near the center of the office space. She held out her hand and closed it into a fist before her as she spoke.

"You can no longer hide from senses most keen,
I banish the shadows to reveal that which cannot be seen."

The air before her shimmered as a wave of magic passed through the room. In its wake, it left the figures of the two Fate sisters standing together in the room, staring intently at Torie.

Jasmin stared at them aghast. "You've been here all this time?"

"You dare use your hex magic on us like that!" said Vera, curtly. "We are Fates! And as such we stand above ——"

Torie cut her off with a wave of her hand. "Enough. I don't know what you are, and the time for games is over. My son is in danger…and you're going to tell us exactly what is going on and what you know. Otherwise. I'm turning you over to that thing that has been hunting you."

Corin's eyes grew large. "You wouldn't."

Now it was Jasmin who spoke up, not bothering to

contain her anger. "Try us." Her eyes glowed and they could feel her power reverberate in the air. "Start talking."

"We don't know where your son is," said Vera. "And that's the truth."

"Why didn't you help protect them?" demanded Torie.

"We could not risk it. The agents of the demon are many, and another could have attacked at any moment," replied Corin.

"And you couldn't chance a second one of you being killed, could you?" said Torie.

The sisters eyed her in surprise. Vera narrowed her eyes at the witch. "You've been in contact with Nerian, haven't you? Has he turned you against us?"

Torie was fuming as she stabbed her finger in the air, pointing to the window. "It doesn't have to turn me against you; you're doing a fine job of that yourself. That monster out there is pure evil, and right now one of its minions has my son. Where are they?"

Vera sighed deeply. "We don't know. And that's the truth. I swear it on my eyes."

In exasperation, Torie slammed her hand on the table, causing the room to vibrate and shudder in response. The two Fates looked around in awe as various bric-a-brac fell from the shelves.

"Tell her," said Corin softly, as she looked at her sister.

"Tell me what?" asked Torie, her voice and temper rising with each passing second.

"We don't know where the shifter has taken your son. But it won't be to the demon," said Vera.

"How do you know that?" asked Jasmin.

"Because he is my bartering chip."

Torie recognized the voice immediately and spun around to see the demon standing in the doorway to her office. She summoned a shield and placed it between the demon and everyone else in the room. Jasmin was at her side instantly, a glowing bubble of orange magic encasing her hands as she held them before her.

"Nerian…" said Corin, her voice a little more than a whisper.

The demon stared at them, the smile he had shown Torie was gone, replaced by a scowl as he regarded the old women. His voice was cold and deep, carrying with it the promise of death.

"Hello, sisters."

Chapter Twenty-Three

All eyes were on the demon and slowly shifted to the Fate sisters, waiting for their response.

"Demon! Most foul of all creations how dare you?" seethed Corin.

Torie flinched at the woman's tone. She had never heard such hatred in anyone's voice before. The words trembled in the air, venom dripping from each sharply articulated word.

"How dare you, sisters, involve these mortals in our affairs. And you think that you can so easily replace me? After the eons we have spent as one, you think a hex witch can take my place? And one of such weak heritage, no less." Nerian smiled now, those perfect white teeth gleaming in stark contrast to the darkness the creature radiated. "Did you even tell her?"

Torie's eyes darted from one to the other as she took in the conversation. "Right now, I don't care about any of this. Where is my son?"

There was a warning growl that rumbled through the space, reverberating off the walls. Elric, in his full wolf form, entered the room, his glowing yellow eyes locked on the demon's form.

"Oh good," said Nerian. "The gang's all here it seems."

Elric leapt, claws extended, mouth full of razor sharp fangs open. But instead of landing on the demon, he passed through its form, landing harmlessly next to the Fates as he shook his head in confusion.

The demon smiled, nodding at Torie. "You didn't think I'd show up here in the flesh, did you? I owe you my thanks for teaching me that little trick."

"How did you find us?" asked Vera.

Nerian nodded in Torie's direction. "When she visited me in her spirit form, I had a feeling that wherever her body lay was where I would find the two of you. So, while she was busy interrogating me, I sent my own disciple in search of her. And wouldn't you know it? Good old Officer Terrance knew exactly where she would be. And he was right. He marked the space for me with a magical lure that he released when he attacked you——" he motioned to Jasmin with a flourish, "——and that was all I needed to find this place. Nice job with the wards by the way. I doubt even I could have found it without help."

"You cannot harm us in that form," said Corin. "You are little more than a ghost."

"True. But now I know where you are," replied Nerian as he turned to Torie. "Of course, you can make this so much easier on everyone. You know where to find me. Bring me my sisters, and I promise no harm will come to your child. Refuse me...well, I think you know what that means."

"Sister, stop this," said Vera. "There may still be a way to work through this."

Nerian laughed, throwing back his head. "You think I want to come back to you? To go back to being enslaved?"

"Enlightenment is not enslavement," said Vera.

Nerian ignored her, looking instead at Torie. "I wouldn't take too much time deciding. Terrance is not quite as stable as I'd like. I really can't be responsible for what might befall your boy after a certain amount of time."

His form started to waver at that moment, a mirage in the summer heat as he began to fade away.

Torie leapt forward, throwing both arms in his direction. "No! You're not going anywhere." A bubble of magic formed around the demon as she gritted her teeth, determined to hold him in place.

Jasmin joined her, adding her own magic to Torie's as she turned toward her friend. "Revelation!" she said between gritted teeth.

Torie nodded and together the two witches spoke in unison.

"Spirits of the moon, hear our plea,
holdfast this creature that seeks to flee.
We ask that all shadows be rent and torn,
and reveal to us now, this monster's true form."

"No!' the demon howled as the power of their hex washed over its body. Magic crackled in the air as it struck the demon, preventing it from becoming incorporeal.

The magic went beyond just holding the dark being in place. It pulled at the ghostly form, branching outward into the world outside Torie's house. The witches watched, maintaining their concentration as their lips moved, invoking the spell again and again to do their bidding.

Everyone in the room watched in wonder as a second, transparent figure was slowly pulled into the room, bound by arcane light as it struggled against the pull of forces beyond its understanding. Slowly, almost painfully, the second figure was pulled into the bubble of magic with the first. Despite their struggles the two were brought together and fused into one. And when it was done, Torie dropped her concealment bubble to reveal the form of an elderly woman, one who glared hatefully at her and her two sisters.

"Fatima," said Vera, her voice little more than a whisper.

"What the——" started Fionna, her own voice filled with confusion.

"You have made a grave error, witch. Bringing me here, revealing my true nature like this? Your mistake," said the woman between heavy breaths.

"And your mistake was threatening us on our own turf," replied Torie. "Everything about this house was designed and built to store and amplify magic. You should have stayed hidden in the woods."

She raised her hand, summoning magic to her.

The demon now known as Fatima raised a hand, giving her that awful smirk that Torie would have recognized no matter the creature's form or sex. "And you're forgetting your son. If Terrance doesn't hear from me soon…"

Torie wavered; the power she had summoned thinned as she took a step forward. She looked out towards the woods before turning her attention back to the demon.

The creature smiled again. "Maybe, if you split yourself again, you might be able to defeat Terrance *and* me…"

Jasmin's hand on her arm got Torie's attention. "Torie, it will take us both to stop this demon, and you know that."

"But…that shifter has Shawn…I can't leave him…"

"You don't have to." It was Elric's voice that rang out to her. He was standing in human form next to them. "You deal with this situation. I'll go bring your son back to you. I promise."

"Oh, good luck with that," sneered the demon. "You and your pal could barely hold your own against my bear. Terrance is on a whole different level. You won't stand a chance alone."

"He won't be alone," said Fionna, nodding at Elric.

The wolf gave Torie's arm a squeeze, and in a flash shifted to his full wolf form and sprinted out of the house. As he passed her by, Fionna shifted into her squirrel form and leapt onto his back. In the blink of an eye, they were racing across the back of the yard and over the iron fence, out of view. Elric had the leopard shifter's scent and Torie knew he would either save her son or die trying.

No.

She pushed the thought from her mind. That wasn't going to happen. He would save Shawn, and everything would be okay.

Turning back to the trapped demon, she gave her a hard look. "Why? You're one of them. Your job is to maintain the balance...not tip the scales towards darkness."

The woman sneered, her upper lip drawing away from jagged old teeth. "I *was* one of them. But I saw the light, so to speak."

"You mean you listened to the dark one...let him whisper in your ear," said Corin. "In siding with that evil, you betrayed us."

"That evil?" said the demon, "Is that what you call him now? You both had the same opportunity I had, and you passed." She stared in Torie's direction. "After everything that happened, you are still willing to bring her into this. Did you tell her why?"

Vera snapped, turning on the woman. "Your betrayal

has nothing to do with her, sister. You left us to go serve the dark…to help free it."

Torie felt a push against her barrier. The demon was slowly exerting power inside the containment sphere, testing the limits of the witches' powers.

"Ugh," Torie said. "Jasmin, she's trying to——"

"Yeah, I feel it," replied her friend. "Just stay focused."

A roar split the room as the gigantic bear shifter entered. It huffed at the witches, swinging its mammoth head from side to side.

"What? Didn't think I'd send for back up?" said the old woman from inside her mystic cage. "Kill the Fates."

Before anyone could act, the bear lunged at the two Fate sisters, one large paw descending on the two women, and all they could do was scream.

Chapter Twenty-Four

With a roar that shook the room, the bear launched a blow that would have split the women in half had it made contact.

Torie made sure that did not happen. She altered her power, casting a glowing bubble around the bear's paw, then, with a sharp yank, pulled downward and then up with her hand, throwing the bear backwards. The demon took advantage of the distraction to throw a hail of fire at the wall of magic binding her.

Jasmin yelled in pain as the barrier slowly burned away. The demon smiled as the wall of magic dropped, leaving Jasmin in its sights. As powerful as she was, even Jasmin knew that her hex magic was limited against such a creature, and before she could erect another shield, the demon threw a blast of fire at her meant to incinerate her where she stood.

All Jasmin could do was throw an arm over her face, hoping the end would come quickly.

Only the fire didn't reach her. Instead, it met resistance

in the form of green fire that countered it midair. Leo was hovering in front of Jasmin, his own dragon fire battling that of the demon. Taking full advantage, Jasmin quickly maneuvered to stand next to Torie, who had pressed herself against one wall, readying for a second attack from the bear.

"Neither of us are going to be able to take on that she-demon alone, and it looks like the Fates are not going to be any help," Jasmin said, nodding in the direction of the sisters. The two of them had shrunk back into a corner and were staring intently at the action taking place around them. "We can't be split up."

Torie was breathing hard. "But the bear…"

Jasmin gave her a quick look and then one to Leo.

Torie swallowed hard, knowing it was the best way, but still terrified by the thought. Finally, she nodded and cast a thought in the dragon's direction.

"Leo…take the bear out…"

Instantly, the little dragon gave a roar that had she not been there, Torie would not have believed came from his tiny frame. He swooped around, banking in the air, and headed for the shifter.

That gave Torie and Jasmin time to flank the demon, approaching from both sides.

"You know, a little help would be nice," said Jasmin to the Fates.

The sisters only looked at her but did not speak.

"Ha. They are forbidden from acting on this plane," said the demon. "It was their impotence that allowed this to happen."

The creature held up a hand and watched as it slowly morphed from that of an old woman's to something gnarled and twisted, blackened and hard. The demon flinched as the burned flesh crept upward, extending across its body until the whole of it appeared as a dark, ashen ember with tiny sparks of orange flame bursting forth from cracks along its surface.

"You see, sisters? This is what I have become." The voice emanating from the creature was like nails dragged over a chalkboard. It raised the flesh along Torie's arms, and it was all she could do not to cover her ears with her hands at the sound.

"Fatima, no!" said Vera, her words breaking into sobs.

"She is no longer our sister," said Corin, the slightest hint of tears in her eyes. She turned to Torie. "She has willfully given over her body and soul to the demon. You have to——" A crack of light and blast of heat sent the two sisters tumbling backwards into the wall.

"No!" Torie screamed, throwing her own magic in the form of a pop of blinding light, at the demon.

As she ran to their aid, Jasmin lifted both hands. A ghostly, blowing chain formed between them as her lips moved, soundlessly invoking an incantation. A second chain formed around the demon, throwing itself in coils around it as Jasmin pulled the chain between her hands taunt.

The demon struggled, throwing more fire at the binds, causing not only the ones encircling her to glow, but also the phantom one in Jasmin's hands. The witch winced with the pain but held fast, refusing to let her conjured chains dissipate.

Torie reached the sisters, bending down to cradle Corin's head. There were burns down the side of her face and body that appeared to slowly be healing, but the woman still gasped for breath. Breathing a spell of comfort and healing across her, Torie gently placed her head onto the floor.

She looked up at Vera. "This is serious, Vera. Whatever

your sister has now become could kill us all. What was Corin going to tell me?"

Torie's eyes were on her friend, fighting for her life as the Fate leaned down and whispered in her ear. Torie's eyes widened and she nodded slowly before making her way to her feet.

"Keep an eye on her," she said to Vera.

Just outside, through the set of doors connecting the study to the large patio, she could hear the sound of battle between the bear shifter and Leo. She chanced a glance outside and saw the bear standing on its hind legs, swatting at the little dragon as Leo zipped nimbly about, staying just out of reach of those razor-sharp paws while simultaneously flitting in close enough to slice the bear with the tip of his wings.

Death by a thousand cuts, thought Torie. She wanted to run to his side but realized that would leave Jasmin alone. There was a greater evil than the bear shifter to deal with, and though she was afraid for the little dragon, she knew where her attention was needed.

Just in time, she turned towards the demon who was in the process of breaking free of the chains Jasmin had entrapped her within. Just as the chains snapped in a shatter of bright, glowing magic, Torie struck.

"In the name of the Gemini, I leave no space to run,
let those that were two now forever be one."

She clapped her hands together forcefully in front of her, sending the incantation forward to strike the demon. Nerian was bowled over with the force of the magic, falling to one knee.

"What have you done?" the demon asked, staring intently at one of its hands.

"Just truly giving you what you claim to have done," Torie said, moving to stand next to Jasmin. "You may have absorbed the essence of the Fate sister known as Fatima, but you lied about absorbing her body. At least you haven't entirely absorbed it. I just hastened that process along a little."

The demon stood, directing its anger at the witches. "What you've done is hasten your own deaths, and then that of the Fates."

"You can appear to us in many different guises in this realm," continued Torie, "But you only take the true physical form of humans. Because we are easy to kill; and our death doesn't really alter your essence. It doesn't hurt you. But you only took the appearance and the essence of Fatima. Why didn't you absorb her body?"

The demon narrowed its eyes at her before glancing at the Fates. "Do your worst witch. I am beyond your ability to harm."

"Maybe," said Torie. "If you were truly in your demon's form, that might be true." She held out her hand. "Salt!"

Her hex power of calling brought the box of salt from the pantry to her hand in a flash. She handed it to Jasmin, nodding.

Jasmin smiled, understanding what they had to do. She began to walk in a circle around the demon, spreading the salt in a solid line as she walked.

"May the lines of ley empower this spell,
and lock this monster within our cell."

As the salt ring began to glow, the demon became

enraged. Slamming its hand onto the ground, it brought forth an eruption of fire that shot out and up in all directions but was completely contained within the circle Jasmin created.

Again, the creature roared in defiance, now slamming its fists against the invisible barrier containing it. "You can't hold me forever. And when I get out, I promise to make all of you pay for this indignity."

Torie walked over to stand just outside the circle of salt. "You're right. This won't hold you forever. Honestly, it doesn't have to." She held out her hand and whispered.

The black blade flew from the large bookshelf to her hand. The demon's eyes grew large at the sight of the knife.

"That belongs to me," the creature growled. "You can't hurt me with it."

"Maybe. But my magic has bound you to the physical shell of the Fate whose essence you absorbed. So, I'm betting you're a little more susceptible to this than you thought. You also said it could be used to cut through the veil that separated our worlds. That solves two problems at once for us."

The demon tried to step back but could not escape the containment spell. Torie held out her hand, palm up, and the black knife flew through the air, lodging itself deep in the demon's chest. The monster howled in rage and true pain but, try as it might, it could not pull the blade free.

Torie moved to stand next to Jasmin, holding her hand as they chanted.

> *"Unclean spirit from beyond the veil,*
> *we cast you back from whence you hail.*
> *Return to the netherworlds so grim,*
> *never again to darken this realm."*

Instantly, spears of light began to erupt through the demon's skin, splitting the blackness as it worked its way out. The demon howled, trying desperately to hold on to its form.

Reaching a hand out towards the Fates, it screamed at the two women. "Sisters! Don't let this happen." But it was no use. The women only stared, watching as the air around the demon split open, pulling it backwards into a nether verse of swirling darkness. The demon squinted, focusing one last time on Torie. "I'll be seeing you again, sister. I'll say hello to our father for you…"

And with that, the monster was gone. Swallowed in a flash of light into another dimension, the rift in the air where it had once been closing in a pop of light, leaving behind only the hollow twang of the black knife hitting the floor where it had once stood.

Torie stood there; her lips pressed into a thin line as she turned towards the Fates. "You mind telling me just what that thing meant by that?"

Chapter Twenty-Five

There wasn't time for answers as a great bellow came from outside on the patio.

"Leo!" Torie cried as she raced outside, magic at the ready.

She reached the door, Jasmin at her side, just in time to see the bear shifter on his back, paws up as he fought vainly to hold the little dragon at bay. The bear was bleeding from a multitude of slashes all over his body and roared in feeble attempt to fend off Leo.

He took in a deep breath, filling his lungs, waiting for the shifter to again roar in his face. As soon as the bear opened its maw, Leo exhaled sharply, sending a blast of dragon fire into the beast's mouth. There was a sudden gasp and rasping that echoed from the bear before its head lapsed to one side, face and head burned to the bone.

Leo hopped off the bear, licked at his wings lazily, then hopped into the air to make his way to Torie's shoulder where he landed lightly with a sigh.

"Well, guess you didn't need any help after all," Torie said, scratching the little one under the chin.

"Mom!"

Torie felt her heart stop as she spun to see her only son. Elric and Fionna had returned, leaping over the railing, Shawn cradled in Elric's arms. As soon as Elric sat him down, he sprinted towards his mother, grabbing her up in a hug that threatened to break her ribs.

Torie smiled, hugging him back as Elric and Fionna approached. Another figure followed them over the railing, and she felt a surge of relief at the sight of Max.

"That leopard put up quite the fight," said Elric. "But in the end, he was just out-classed by your man."

Fionna cleared her throat, followed by a forced cough into her hand.

"Well, okay...your man, his best friend, and one of the fiercest little squirrel fighters I've ever seen in my life," Elric continued.

"Max, how did you find them?" Torie asked.

The big sheriff shrugged. "Blame it on the pheromones, I guess. I could smell Elric in the air...and could tell by the amount of stress he was giving off that something wasn't right. So, I tracked him."

"I can't thank you enough for bringing my boy home safe," she said, her voice cracking. "I never doubted you for a moment." This time she stared directly at Elric, her eyes beginning to overflow with wetness.

"Mom! You'll never guess! I used my powers! That shifter went to bite me right before Elric showed up, and... bam...I hit him with something! It felt like my mind was on fire and I just threw it all at the leopard. Knocked him for a loop. You should have seen it."

Torie frowned. "We can discuss that later. Now I'm just

glad you're back safe and sound. Did that shifter hurt you at all? Fionna, can you call Glen and maybe even Emil to look him over?"

Shawn started to protest, but one look told him not to even try it.

As they all headed back into the house, Elric cast a sideways glance at the half-melted bear on the patio. "Looks like you guys did okay as well."

Once inside, Torie walked over to where Jasmin was attending the Fate sisters, holding a wet cloth to Corin's head.

"Is she going to be alright?" asked Torie.

"As far as I can tell. She's a tough one, that's for sure."

Torie nodded, offering a slight smile. "Vera, what was that demon talking about?"

The Fate opened her mouth to speak, but then seemed to think better of it and snapped it closed.

"Oh no. I just saved your life and those of your disciples. You can at least tell me what that crack about my father was about."

"I will tell you, but first…you still have work to do."

Torie stared at her, perplexed. "What work? We defeated the demon; sent it back to who knows where."

"We know where it was sent. And we also know there is still a way for it to return at some point…" Vera answered cryptically.

"The Devil's Tramping Grounds," said Jasmin softly.

Vera nodded. "You need to sanctify it; seal it with your hex power. And it needs to be done sooner rather than later."

Together, they stood beside the dead patch of earth known as the Devil's Tramping Grounds. With a very carefully worded incantation, the pit had been consecrated in the language of the hexes and wrapped in a powerful cocoon of magic that worked its way deep into the bitter soil.

Jasmin breathed a long sigh of relief. "Well, I don't know if anything will ever grow there again, but one thing's for sure; nothing should come crawling out of it again anytime soon."

Torie nodded in agreement. "But just to be on the safe side, we leave the trails leading here closed. I would feel better knowing no one ever wanders upon this area again."

"So that's how you work your magic, huh? It's just rhyming words and then, poof, it happens? Can I try?" Shawn asked.

"No!" both Jasmin and Torie responded in unison.

"We will talk about this when we get home," said Torie. "For now, I just want to get out of here. This place still gives me the creeps, and I'm sure Elric has worn a hole in the floor with all his pacing by now."

Despite all the protests, everyone finally agreed it was not a good idea for the shifters to get too close to the pit just yet.

"Shawn, run ahead and wait at the car. I need to chat with your mom for a minute." Jasmin slid an arm through Torie's as they watched Shawn trot ahead of them, back to the car where the Fate sisters were waiting. "You know that man loves you so much."

Torie stopped, looking at her friend. "And I love him just as much. But you said that almost as if it were a warning to me."

Jasmin pursed her lips. "Well, sometimes, holding something you love at bay can be just as harmful as holding it too tightly. You can't treat him like he's something that needs to be protected all the time. We run into a lot of serious situations…he's here to help you and has proved that more times than we can count."

They continued walking and Torie breathed a deep sigh. "You're right. As much as I may like to think otherwise, I can't do it all. I also learned I can't be everywhere at once. I'm just so afraid of him getting hurt. Or you. Or Fionna…or…" she couldn't bring herself to finish the words.

"Or Shawn? Hey, the worst happened and he's okay."

Torie patted her friend's hand. She looked ahead as they broke into the clearing near the gravel parking lot where Jasmin's SUV was parked. The sisters were standing outside the car, speaking with Shawn. The young man was nodding, and as they approached, everyone grew quiet.

"Was it successful?" asked Vera.

"Well, maybe if you had come with us, you would have been able to see for yourself," said Jasmin.

Torie cleared her throat. "What she means is, yes, we believe the pit has been sealed. Time will tell."

"Indeed, it will," said Corin, eyeing her sister.

"Okay, what is going on?" asked Torie.

Vera exhaled sharply before speaking up. "My sister is injured. She needs rest and proper care; the kind of care that I can't give her here. It is time for us to return to our own realm."

"What? That wasn't part of the deal," said Torie. "We came out here to seal the pit and then you tell me what I need to know."

Vera smiled; her normally bright eyes were heavy from a lack of sleep. "Fatima was lured to the darkness over time. It didn't just happen overnight. It was a slow progression; a cancer that grew in her over centuries. It's a pull that all of us have felt, but we resist."

"We felt it because beings such as us share a commonality. We evolved, over many, many years, from the same source, so to speak," continued Corin. "It is the duality of nature that we represent...the light and the dark."

"And in our sister's case, the gray," said Vera. "She was seduced by the whisperings of the dark ones. She grew weary of our pledge to maintain balance, and to only observe. She wanted to help shape man's destiny; and once she allowed that desire an opening, the dark one knew exactly how to take advantage of her. She strayed from her path willingly...and as such suffered the price."

"But why did she call me sister?" Torie asked. "And that crack about my father..."

The sisters exchanged looks. "She was referring to the fact that hex magic is a form of witchcraft that comes from the other realm...the one that we inhabit. You are a kindred spirit so to speak. Your heritage is from our world."

Both Jasmin and Torie were stunned into silence.

"That isn't true," said Jasmin. "Our power comes from the earth itself."

Vera smiled. "Perhaps. But which Earth?"

"Tell me, Torie Bliss, what do you know about your father? Consider this; your gifts as a hex witch are prodigious. Greater than any we have ever witnessed. Maybe you should investigate where that came from," said Corin.

Torie opened her mouth to speak but was cut off by Vera's sharply raised hands. "No more questions. We have much to do and little time to do it in, I'm afraid. But there is one last thing we need from you. We still need a third Fate. Without that, the scales are unbalanced and will eventually tip in favor of the dark again. It's only a matter of time before another demon slips through the veil and enters your world. When Fatima left us, that was when the wall separating our realms weakened enough to let Nerian slip through. Without a third sister…"

"Nerian was right in one aspect; the ability to become one of us is in your blood," said Corin.

Jasmin stepped forward, eyes blazing. "She already said she isn't going with you."

Vera nodded. "Yes. She made that very clear. And in truth, after what we have witnessed, we can see that your place is here. This town, this realm, needs you. But we have a need as well."

Torie shook her head slowly. "I'm sorry. I'm not leaving my friends."

Corin cocked her head to one side. "We know. But we weren't talking to you."

Torie felt her heart stop as she followed the gaze of both sisters as they landed on her son. Power flared to life around her as magic crackled in the air. Blue flames flowed around Jasmin as she lifted both hands into the air, her eyes growing pale as she tapped into her hex abilities.

Torie's voice, deepened by power she had never tapped into before, sounded foreign in her ears. "You will not touch him."

The Fates backed up, and Shawn stepped between the four women, raising his arms. "Mom, it's okay. They aren't going to make me do anything against my will."

Torie stopped, her magic cycling down slowly as his meaning sank in.

"They talked to me about it on the ride over…and I agreed."

"What? They spoke to you in the car? Is that why all of

you were so quiet on the ride over?" asked Jasmin. "Telepathy, I assume."

"It doesn't matter how," Shawn said. "The fact is, they can teach me how to use powers that I don't even understand. Mom, seeing you in action, seeing what you can do... it's made me realize that this is what I want to do as well. I've been floundering lately, feeling so adrift and not knowing why. But now, being exposed to all of this, it's like my eyes have been opened for the first time. This is what I'm meant to do."

Torie's mouth was open, yet no words would come. Only tears flowed from her as her entire being threatened to shut down in pain.

"But you're all I have..."

"Torie. He will be safe with us. I promise you that," said Vera, softly. "Safer than any place in your world. And yes, you will see him again. Many, many times, I promise you. Think of it as him going off to a new college; one that will help him become who he's truly meant to be. And it will help keep you and this realm safe."

Torie turned to her son. "This...is something you really want? Of your own free will?"

He smiled radiantly, lighting up his mother's broken heart. "More than anything." He stepped back to stand next to the sisters. "I love you, Mom. Always and forever. And I'll see you soon."

"Tell the disciples to return to their homes and await our next contact," said Vera. "They have a new Fate to get to know after all..."

With that, her voice faded into the distance as their forms began to shimmer. Sparkles of green floated in the air around them, obscuring them in a vortex of light, until finally, they were gone. Leaving only the silence of the forest and the sobs of a mother behind.

Chapter Twenty-Six

Torie sat in a rocking chair on the patio, looking at the setting sun over the hills. She drew the down blanket closer around her as she sipped a small tumbler of whiskey. The hum of the cicadas and the blinking of the fireflies cast a spell that only nature could create.

"You okay?" asked Elric as he pulled up a chair next to her.

She smiled, placing an arm on his knee and leaning her head onto his shoulder. "I just...I feel like a bad mother. I'm supposed to protect him from danger; not send him off into it."

Elric shifted so she had to look up into his eyes. He cupped her chin lovingly in his hand. "Hey. Maybe, in doing what you did and letting him go, you've protected him in a way no one ever could. I mean, I love Singing Falls, but would you really want him learning how to use his magic in this environment?"

Torie sighed and moved her head back to his shoulder.

"You might have a point there. I don't trust the Fates, but they have every reason to keep him alive and safe."

The sound of drawers slamming and something hitting the floor caught their attention. Torie laughed, shaking her head.

"Well, the good thing about having a magical house that cleans itself is the fact that it makes straightening up after a demon and bear shifter attack so much easier."

Elric laughed, laying his head on hers.

"Thank you again, for bringing him home. I don't know what I would have done if——"

"Don't. There is no need to go there. Ever. You know I will always have your back. What you love, I love."

She sighed, snuggling in closer, feeling the heat his body gave off. "So, we're good?"

He kissed the top of her head. "Better than good."

"That's good to know. Because I'm going to need your help soon."

"Let me guess; you need a lot of boxes lifted as the bakery is being readied for its grand opening?"

Now it was Torie's turn to laugh. "No. Not that. Besides, Fionna is a lot stronger than she looks. We got that handled. But I was talking with Jasmin and there are a couple of things we need to figure out moving forward."

"Such as?"

Torie took a deep breath. "For one thing, we need to find out how her daughter came to possess a knife that belonged to a demon. That means trying to track her down as well as Jasmin's sister, Opal."

Elric frowned. The last time those two had come to town it had been to kill Elric and Max.

"And the second thing?" he asked.

Torie took a deep breath. "I need to find out more about my father. He wasn't a part of my life growing up, and my mother always refused to talk about him. Now I know there's a reason why. And as unpleasant as it may be, I need you to help me find out who…or *what*…he is."

vinci-books.com/hexafterdark

A moonlit quest for a rare herb turns deadly in Singing Falls.

Torie and her friends must uncover sinister secrets to save their town from an evil coven. *Hex After Dark*—the magic has never been darker.

Turn the page for a free preview…

Hex After Dark: Chapter One

Trudging through two inches of muck that threatened to pull her shoes off was not how Torie Bliss had envisioned her evening going. She frowned at her best friend Jasmin's back as they made their way through the lowland bog, the moonlight glinting off the metal of her gardening tools. "Let's go harvest some plants, they said...it will be fun, they said," Torie grunted. "And in case it wasn't clear, you are the *they* that said this."

Jasmin waved her hand over her shoulder. "Yeah, yeah, so I've heard. But you didn't exactly protest too much when I brought the idea up." She stopped, hands on hips, as she gulped some deep breaths. "As a matter of fact, if I remember right, you said there was no better time than the present to make it happen."

They were out in the middle of the night, on a steep hillside leading to a plateau where a very specific plant grew. It was one they needed for a very specific spell they had discovered in one of Torie's mother's grimoires.

Torie frowned. "Yes, well that was before I knew it was

going to cost me my favorite pair of hiking boots. I'll never get all this mud off them."

"Well, what is the point of having them if you're not actually going to wear them?"

Torie blinked rapidly at her friend. "I wear them. Just not out in the mud and dirt. They're too nice for all that."

Jasmin chuckled, took a deep breath, and started moving forward again. "Come on, we have to find that lunarwort. It only blooms under a full moon and we only have two hours before it's gone."

Torie sighed and followed her friend, her boots squelching in the mud. She looked up at the moon, a giant orb in the night sky, and said a silent prayer that they would find what they were looking for.

"And what kind of plant only blooms for a couple of hours a night, once a month? Who came up with that?" she mumbled.

"A magic one, obviously," answered Jasmin as they crested the hill, coming to an open field before them.

The light of the full moon broke across the open space like a shimmering silver carpet. There was very little wind to disturb the growth, and the stillness of the stems of the reeds and large grasses only added to the feeling of serenity the two witches could only admire in awe.

"Alright," said Jasmin. "The lunarwort should be growing on the other side of this field. We should have about an hour to harvest some before it goes dormant for another month."

Torie nodded and followed her friend, their eyes scanning the expanse before them for the telltale glimmer of the plant. Somewhere in the distance, or maybe it came from behind them, an owl hooted, followed by the sound of large, ruffled wings disturbing the silence. Torie started, looking over her shoulder then up at the star-filled sky.

"That was an owl, Torie," said Jasmin. She hadn't even bothered to look back at her friend.

"What kind of owl is that big? Who knows what that could have been."

"Barn owls can have a wingspan of up to four feet." Jasmin stopped and turned to her friend, a twinkle in her eyes. "Or it could have been an owl-shifter. Who knows how big those can get."

Torie swallowed hard, her eyes darted to and fro.

Jasmin laughed softly as they continued. "Oh, calm down. Why are you so jumpy? You've fought vampires, golems and all manner of demons before. But now you're afraid of an owl?"

Torie huffed. "I'm not afraid. I just don't like being out here in the dark. It's so wide open and we are exposed. Anything could attack us, plus, we can't see in the dark."

"Hah. It's nighttime, but it's not dark out. There is a difference. Not a cloud in the sky to obscure the moonlight. And besides, we have this." She held out one hand and produced a ball of shimmering, blue magic that bounced across the field before disappearing in a soft pop of iridescent fireworks.

Torie felt a tingle in the back of her head, a pulling sensation that tickled just under her scalp.

"Wait, Jasmin, do that again."

Her friend gave her a questioning look, but did as she asked, producing another ball of magic and sending it sailing across the field.

There was definitely a reaction this time. Torie wasn't sure where it came from, or what it was, and she looked around puzzled.

"What is it?" asked Jasmin.

"I'm not sure. Didn't you feel that? Something reacted to your magic. It was like a whisper that I felt, instead of heard."

Jasmin looked around, studying the field and the tree line on the far side. She sent her senses outward, feeling for anything that could account for the type of disturbance Torie was feeling. "I don't feel anything."

"It's gone now. It was only there when you sent your magic out."

Jasmin squinted in the distance. "It could have just been the area itself, responding to magical energy. This area is known to collect and hold power. That's why the lunarwort grows here, and only here. The soil is rich with primal energies. Witches have been coming here for generations to practice moon magic."

Torie smiled. "Good old Singing Falls. A surprise in every nook and corner."

They continued, and as they reached the far side of the field, they got their first look at the mystic plant for which they had undertaken a mile's-long hike in the middle of the night.

"And that," said Jasmin, pointing, "is what we came for."

There, before the field ended and broke into the line of pine trees where the forest started, were the most beautiful plants Torie had ever seen. The lunarwort was a small, delicate flower, growing to a height of about five inches, with a petite white blossom and slender green stem. Its petals were dusted with a silvery, moonlight sheen, and the center of the flower was illuminated with a brilliant golden hue. Torie thought she detected a gentle, ethereal fragrance carried in the air around it, like a soft whisper of enchantment. The leaves curved gracefully, reaching upward to the sky in clusters. Moonlight bathed them and caused a rippling effect to pass through the leaves in a light show that drew the witches' eyes. The closer Torie and Jasmin stepped to them, the more the flowers shimmered in response.

"So pretty," Torie said. "It's almost a shame to pick them." She looked over at her friend, who seemed to be studying the ground around the flowers with a frown. "What's wrong?"

Jasmin placed a hand on her chin in thought. "I'm not sure. They don't look quite right. They should be taller and growing much closer together. As a matter of fact, there should be many more of them. Half of the field should be covered in them, not just this one section."

"Are they affected by temperature extremes or anything like that? It's been unseasonably cold the last couple of weeks," Torie said.

Jasmin shook her head. "No. Lunarwort thrives on magic. The weather has no effect on them at all." She reached out a glowing hand, holding it towards the plants. In response, they stretched in her direction, their shimmer turning into a lightship of glittering beauty. "They seem fine, however. Maybe I'm just remembering them wrong. It's been years since I've been up here during a full moon." She shrugged. "We don't have long, so time to harvest."

"And you're sure removing them from the ground won't hurt them?"

"They will be fine. In another hour they will recede back into the earth, recharging, and waiting to spring forth again next month. The blossoms are filled with the power we need for the spell. Once we harvest them, the energy will go dormant, until it's mixed with the rest of the ingredients called for."

She reached for her gardening shears and trowel, handing the tiny shovel to Torie.

"Loosen the earth around them and then pull the plant free root and all. Try not to damage the stalk. Unlike most plants, removing the root is what allows new ones to grow in their place."

They set about harvesting the plant, taking care not to damage the delicate leaves. Jasmin began to hum slightly as they gathered the flowers and placed them in the cloth satchels each carried.

Torie smiled as the flowers pulsed in cadence with Jasmin's voice. "You really do have a way with plants. I wish I had your green thumb—" She stopped, her body stiffening.

Jasmin stopped humming. "Are you feeling it again?"

Torie nodded. "For just a second, yes. But it was stronger that time." She stood, adjusting her satchel. "It's definitely coming from...there." She pointed to an area to their right where a patch of the field faded away before leading into a section of bushy overgrowth just before the tree line began. "I may not have your way with plants, but something is off about the ground in that direction."

"Agreed," said Jasmin. "I can feel it now as well. Come on."

Together, they moved cautiously in the direction Torie had indicated. They stopped when they reached an area of heavy overgrowth. The vines and vegetation had intertwined aggressively, interweaving with roots of all kinds.

"This looks natural...but at the same time unnatural," said Jasmin. She closed her eyes and held out her hands as she began to chant.

"Let the plants of this place lift the veil of secrecy,

so the truth may be revealed and made known to me."

In response, the ground heaved, and the vegetation shivered before drawing back and separating. The earth roiled and opened as it pushed a body upward into view.

Torie gasped, one hand over her mouth as they drew back.

Even with the face turned away from them, they could tell from the size and the clothing that it was the body of a man, slight of build. Dirt and moss were caked over it, and several centipedes and ants scurried away from the corpse.

"Holy mother! Who would do this?" demanded Torie.

Despite her trepidation, Jasmin peered closer. "This hasn't been here very long. And there are no signs of digging tools where the earth would have been broken to dig a grave." She stood back, staring at her friend, eyes wide. "You know what that means?"

Torie nodded, still not wanting to look at the body. "Magic?"

"Yep. Someone killed him, and then had the ground swallow him up like this. I'm betting that's the disturbance you were sensing."

Torie let out a sigh as she fished her cell phone from one of the pockets of her satchel. "Just once. Just once, I'd like to go for a hike, walk around a corner, walk out of a store...anything; and not run into something horrific."

Jasmin snorted. "You're in the wrong town for that. Calling Max?"

Torie nodded. The town sheriff, who happened to be a werewolf and the best friend of her boyfriend, was going to love this one.

"Might as well tell him to get Emil up here as well. Something tells me he's going to be needed."

Dr. Emil Faun was the resident medical examiner, and sprite, for the county. Unlike Max, he would undoubtedly be excited at the sight of a murder scene like this.

"Is that because you're looking for a reason to see him again?" Torie chided with a smile.

Jasmin averted her eyes, thankful that moonlight would obscure any signs of discomfort. "Just trying to make both their lives easier by getting them here at the same time. While you do that, I'm going to nose around. See if I can find any magical residue that might give us a clue as to what happened."

Torie nodded; her attention captured by the gruff voice on the other end.

"It's the middle of the night and you're calling me. What foulness have you uncovered now?" said Max, his voice filled with sleepiness and annoyance.

"Oh, you hit that one right on the head," Torie said with a sigh.

Hex After Dark: Chapter Two

As expected, Max was in a foul mood, but was also laser focused on everything about the crime scene. His enhanced senses could only pick up the scents of Torie, Jasmin, and the deceased. No sign of whoever had committed the crime. That was in keeping with what Jasmin's magic had told her as well. There was no trace of anyone else being in the area.

Max was crouched down next to the body while furiously scribbling in his notepad as Torie moved to stand next to him.

"Any ideas?" she asked.

He looked up at her and frowned. "Yes. I think you two are magnets for the weird and macabre. Why is it that you are always stumbling onto scenes like this?" I opened my mouth to speak but he held up a hand. "That was rhetorical."

Torie pursed her lips and watched the big sheriff as he studied the body. "Where's Emil?"

"He's on his way. Should be here any minute now," Max answered.

Then, as if on cue, the little sprite emerged from the woods, taking the small group by surprise.

"Doc, where did you come from?" asked Max, his eyes darting to the darkness behind the medical examiner.

Emil Faun frowned, almost as if he didn't understand the question. "From my house of course. You called me, after all."

Max blinked at him. "No, I mean just now. The road is that way—" he motioned behind him with his thumb, "—yet you came out of the—you know what? Never mind. Here's the body, start doing whatever it is you do."

"Hi, Emil." Jasmin had popped up and was standing next to the examiner with her hands clasped behind her back.

His smile reached all the way to his eyes as he nodded. "Hello, Jasmin. It's good to see you." The reason for him to be there seemed to come flooding back to him when Max cleared his throat. "Oh, um...yes. The body. Who found it?"

"We did," said Jasmin, eagerly. "I can tell you whatever you need to know about it."

Max rolled his eyes. "And while you're doing that, I'm going to walk the perimeter. See if I can pick up anything further out."

"I'll go with you," Torie said.

The big wolf grumbled but nodded. Together, they headed off towards the tree line, crossing into the shadowed darkness created by the canopy of growth above them.

"What were you two doing up here anyway?" Max said, walking slowly through the thickets.

"We were harvesting lunarwort. It's a plant that only grows here in the light of the full moon. We're casting a spell I found and it's one of the ingredients."

Max was silent as he surveyed the ground, moving

forward slowly. His body was tense, and Torie could tell he was using all his senses as he swept his gaze across the forest floor.

"Would some light help?" she asked, holding up a hand to create a glowing ball of orangish light.

Max shook his head. "Thanks, but no. I can see perfectly fine in the dark, and the shadows created by your magic are...not natural. It throws off my senses."

Recalling her light, Torie walked on behind him in silence. A branch cracking caused her to jump slightly, and Max turned to her.

"I know," she said, "There's nothing to be afraid of out here that I can't handle."

"Well, true, but that's not what I was going to say. I was going to say that it was just a deer stepping on some twigs to our right while foraging. Nothing more."

Torie took in a deep breath, drawing in the scent of dry pine needles and the musty odor of decaying leaves. She felt comfortable with Max and was thankful for his presence, even if he was grumpy.

He stopped short, squatting down to run his hands over the earth in front of them. He picked up a bit of dirt and sniffed at it.

"What is it?" asked Torie.

He sniffed again before cocking his head to one side, listening intently. "Someone was just here."

And then Torie felt it; the same tickling at the back of her head that she experienced when she and Jasmin were crossing the field. She spun around, and this time cast a swath of magic, a spell designed to illuminate areas hidden by incantation.

The shrubbery behind them rippled and shrank back from her power. Immediately, Max was in wolf form and pounced into the undergrowth, Torie fast on his heels. She could feel whatever had been watching them in retreat, disappearing through the dense foliage at a rapid pace. She tried to cast her thoughts ahead, see if she could get a look at whoever—or whatever—it might have been. But whatever it was, it was bathed in magic that she wasn't familiar with, and it shrugged off her attempts to grasp it with her power.

"Max! It's shifted direction—turned left!" she called to her friend.

With preternatural agility, the big wolf stopped mid-stride and leapt to his left, the woods shaking with the force of his stride as he ran. He quickly pulled away from Torie as she struggled to draw in enough breath to flood her struggling lungs with oxygen. She was so focused on the being they were chasing that she nearly ran into Max's backside when she burst free of the brush.

The wolf had stopped in a small clearing that looked like a game trail and was sniffing the ground heavily.

"Do you still sense them?" he said to her through the mental rapport she shared with all shifters in their non-human form.

She closed her eyes and reached outward, probing the surrounding region. Nothing.

"No," she said, opening her eyes. "Whatever it was, it's just...gone."

Max shimmered in place as he shifted back into his human form. "How can that be? What kind of magic are we facing?"

"No idea. But we better get back to the others. Make sure this wasn't just to draw us away."

Max nodded and they hurried through the woods, Torie trusting Max's unerring senses to guide them back to the crime scene. Both Jasmin and Dr. Faun looked up from studying the body and knew immediately that something was wrong.

"What happened?" said Jasmin, not bothering to mask any concerns she felt for her friend. "Are you okay?"

Torie waved, letting her know they were fine, as she bent over, gathering breath into her still-aching lungs.

"We found signs of someone, or something, watching us from in the woods," said Max. "We tried to chase it down, but it escaped."

Jasmin frowned, her eyes flicking from one to the other. "Do you think it was whoever was responsible for this?" She gestured to the body behind her.

"No idea," said Torie. "But they were definitely magical. Nothing human moves the way this thing did." She glanced at the medical examiner. "Do you believe this was a murder?"

"And if it was a murder, was it committed here or was this just where the body was dumped?" added Max.

"Both excellent questions," said Emil. "And ones that I will have answers to once the body is back at my lab so I can examine it closer. I did find something of interest, but I'd rather not say for certain what it is until I can run a couple of tests. I can say that the body has only been here for a couple of hours before being found."

Torie nodded. "So more likely than not, whatever that was in the woods was either involved or saw what happened."

"Agreed," said Max. "For now, let's get this body back to Dr. Faun's office. I'll come back in the morning with Elric and scout the area farther north of where the trail went cold. See if we can't pick something up."

Jasmin turned to Torie. "Speaking of your man, where is Elric?"

"He was going to run some errands in town earlier tonight and then spend the evening at his place cleaning it up. He's making sure he gets that security deposit back," Torie answered.

Jasmin's eyes lit up. "Oh, that's right. This weekend is the big day. You guys are moving in together." She wiggled her eyebrows lasciviously.

In response, Torie rolled her eyes. "Yes, we will officially be living in sin."

Jasmin smiled. "Please. You know how happy I am for you both. I just can't wait to see how that works out. A witch, a werewolf and a dragon living together in an enchanted house. How fun."

"Might as well be two witches," said Max, "Considering the fact you live right next door to them and are over at Torie's house most of the time."

Jasmin laughed. "Oh, you know I'll be sitting on my porch with a big bowl of popcorn watching it all."

"Ha ha," Torie deadpanned. "Come on, we better get going if we're going to get these lunarworts under cover before daylight breaks."

"Do you need a lift?" asked Max. "Cos otherwise, I'll stay here with the good doc until the medic team can get here to transport the body downtown."

"No, we're fine," said Jasmin as they moved away from the medical examiner. "We're parked just off the main road. It's a straight hike back down for us. You keep an eye on Emil." Her voice dropped until it was barely above a whisper. "If something capable of eluding the two of you is prowling around up here, I don't think he should be left alone."

"Agreed," whispered Torie.

They turned to leave and waved goodbye to Emil. He popped his head up and waved enthusiastically back.

"And thank you for the concern, Jasmin. But I assure you, I can take care of myself." He smiled, and then returned to collecting bits of dirt and placing it carefully in plastic baggies.

"Darned sprite hearing," said Jasmin, shaking her head as they marched off.

They made the descent back to Jasmin's SUV in silence. Once at the car, Torie turned to her friend. "Whatever that was that Max and I chased, is the same thing I sensed watching us as we were trekking through that field."

Jasmin nodded. "Figured as much. But why didn't it attack? Why just watch us? Especially knowing we were more likely than not going to stumble across that body." She unlocked the doors, and they climbed inside.

"No idea," said Torie. "Unless it wanted us to find the body."

"Yeah. That's what I was afraid of."

The night sky was split by a bolt of lightning in the distance, and from habit, Torie counted the seconds until the rumble of thunder hit them.

"Looks like there is a storm coming. With luck, we can get home before the rain," she said.

Jasmin stared out the front window looking up at the sky. "I hope Emil gets everything he needs from the site. It looks like it's going to pour. That will completely wash away any evidence he doesn't collect."

She started the big car's engine and eased out onto the main road that would take them back to their houses just outside of town.

Torie sat silently, staring out the passenger side window.

Her thoughts were on the body they found. Neither of them had recognized the man. He hadn't been dressed for night weather, and certainly didn't appear to have hiked the ridge the way she and Jasmin had. She flashed back to the way the man was bound by the earth, his mouth slightly open and filled with dirt and rotted vegetation. Whoever he was, he deserved better than being consigned to the ground in such a manner.

No matter what Emil's reports were going to say, she was sure of one thing. Someone had killed him up on that mountain. And she was now determined to find out who.

Hex After Dark: Chapter Three

"Come on, I'll show you how to prepare these," Jasmin said, as she threw the car into park outside Torie's house.

They climbed the couple of steps to the large, welcoming front porch leading to double glass doors. Torie reached out with her mind, feeling for the wards protecting her home. Confident they were undisturbed, she dropped them and pushed the door open.

As soon as the stepped into the foyer, Leo came bounding down the hall to greet them. A flap of his leathery wings sent the little dragon airborne and into Torie's arms where he nuzzled his snout against her chest. She ran a hand along the ridge of his head, cooing to him.

"Hello, little one. How's my happy baby tonight? Did you miss me?"

In response the little dragon rested his head against her and let out a puff of smoke that circled Torie's face. She laughed, waving her hand to clear the air. "And here's Auntie Jazzy...she missed you as well."

The dragon flitted from Torie's arms to Jasmin's. She

grunted as he climbed her chest to land on her shoulder, wrapping his tail lovingly around her neck.

"Okay, okay," Jasmin said playfully. "I don't need to go home smelling like a chimney. Go play." She placed the little guy on the floor and watched as he scampered off towards the back of the house where Torie's study was. "He's definitely growing. What are you going to do when he reaches maturity?"

Torie sighed. "I suppose I'll have to build him something bigger out back."

"That's not what I meant. He's a dragon, Torie."

"I know. But...he's my baby. I'll deal with it at some point. But not just yet."

Together, they walked through the spacious kitchen and out the patio doors. It was just starting to rain lightly as they made their way to the greenhouse Torie had built off to one side of the main house. Once inside, they plopped their satchels on the wooden worktable in the center of the space. The warm, humid air was heavy with the sweet scent of blooming flowers and the earthy aroma of fresh potting soil.

Jasmin took in a deep breath. "I love this place. You really outdid yourself."

"Well, I couldn't have done it without you. You've probably forgotten more about plants than I'll ever know."

Jasmin smiled as she took out the lunarwort she had collected and placed it on the table. "And don't you forget it."

Torie placed her own plants next to those of her friend, marveling at the fact that they still looked as fresh as they had when glowing under the moonlight. "Now what?"

"Their power is in the leaves, but they need to be dried just right in order not to let the mystical energies leak out. We need to use a spell that is a combination of healing and thanks, and then hang them upside down on a pegboard made of white oak."

Torie moved to one of the floor-to-ceiling cabinets built into the shed and opened it, retrieving a hardwood board with several holes cut into it.

"Got it," she said, bringing it to the worktable.

"And now, we bind it in place with enchanted spider silk."

Again, Torie shuffled off to the cabinet and retrieved a small wooden box painted red. Inside, she found a spool of gossamer thread that sparkled silver at her touch. She laid it before them on the table and watched as Jasmin picked up a length and wrapped it around the stem of one of the plants. She nodded to Torie to mimic her actions as she secured the plant, leaves down, on the pegboard. As she did, she began to speak.

"I thank you, sister plants, for your service and aide,
may you be entombed in magic, free from harm and dismay."

Torie repeated the incantation and mirrored her friend's actions until all the lunarwort was strung up on the board. Then, Jasmin took the board and stood it up on one end of the table, leaning back against the wall.

"That's pretty much it," she said.

"Now what?" asked Torie.

"Now, we wait. It will take a few days before the leaves are at the right degree of dryness to grind into the powder to create the potion for the spell."

"Good to know. But can I just ask one thing? In light of the tragedy we just uncovered, is now really the best time to be playing around with spells we've never tried before? I mean...I know Max didn't mean anything by it, but he has a point. This type of stuff seems drawn to us. What if experimenting with new spells just amplifies whatever is going on around here?"

She followed Jasmin to the large copper sink at one end of the greenhouse and waited for her friend to wash up before she ran her own hands under the warm water.

Jasmin dried her hands and turned to face Torie. "This is how we learn. How we get better. We have an obligation to this town and this community. We can't just sit back on our laurels and hope we will always be good enough to take on what's always waiting around the next corner. Our enemies aren't waiting. You think whoever or whatever did that to that man on the mountain is sitting back thinking they've done enough? We both know that's not the case. We have to continually grow...otherwise, we're just sitting ducks for the next big bad that comes for us or our loved ones."

Her words hung in the air, waiting to be absorbed. Finally, Torie nodded. "You're right, of course. I just can't help but wonder if all this would be happening if I had never showed up in this town."

Jasmin took both of her friend's hands in hers and stared her in the eye. "Torie, as powerful as we may be, neither of us can answer a question like that. But what I can say is that I would not change a thing that has happened since you came into my life. Because meeting you has been one of my life's greatest joys. You are my best friend, and the sister I would have chosen. I will never question why you're here; I'm just going to be thankful that you are."

Torie meshed her lips tightly as tears threatened to overwhelm her. "Oh stop. You're going to make me cry, and no one wants to see that."

Jasmin pursed her lips. "Yeah, you got that right. You keep that to yourself."

Torie laughed and pulled her friend in for a quick hug. "And right back at you."

They parted and Jasmin let out a sharp exhale. "Alright, I say we try to get whatever sleep we can, then meet and head to town. We can go the bakery as soon as it opens and see how Fionna is doing. She hired those two associates and wants us to meet them."

Torie glanced at her watch, feeling the tug between being at the house when Elric returned and being there for Fionna. Although Torie, Jasmin, and Fionna had worked hard to make the bakery successful, she wasn't sure how well it would be received. It was especially popular with the breakfast crowd, but Torie was uncertain as to just how much community support there would be. She was torn between wanting to be there for Elric and wanting to know how the bakery would do.

"I'll meet you back at the car in thirty minutes. We can't leave our girl hanging."

Grab your copy...
vinci-books.com/hexafterdark

About the Author

M.J. Caan is an avid reader and writer of all things science fiction and fantasy. Author of multiple science fiction and paranormal fantasy series, M.J. likes to think that there is still magic out there in the world. Even if it's only between the pages of a great book.